HOT-SHOT HEROES: BILLIONAIRE DOCTOR, ORDINARY NURSE

Carol Marinelli

MILLS & BOON

First published in Great Britain 2008
by Mills & Boon, an imprint of Harlequin (UK) Limited,
Large Print edition 2012
Harlequin (UK) Limited,
Eton House, 18-24 Paradise Road, Richmond, Surrey TW9 1SR

© Carol Marinelli 2008

ISBN: 978 0 263 23048 2

Harlequin (UK) policy is to use papers that are natural, renewable
and recyclable products and made from wood grown in sustainable
forests. The logging and manufacturing process conform to the
legal environmental regulations of the country of origin.

Printed and bound in Great Britain
by CPI Antony Rowe, Chippenham, Wiltshire

The ultimate kings of seduction!

THE PLAYBOYS
AND HEROES
COLLECTION

The Playboys and Heroes large print collection
gives you lavish stories of luxury
from your favourite top authors
in easier-to-read print.

Carol Marinelli recently filled in a form where she was asked for her job title, and was thrilled, after all these years, to be able to put down her answer as 'writer'. Then it asked what Carol did for relaxation, and after chewing her pen for a moment Carol put down the truth—'writing'. The third question asked—'What are your hobbies?' Well, not wanting to look obsessed or, worse still, boring, she crossed the fingers on her free hand and answered 'swimming and tennis'. But, given that the chlorine in the pool does terrible things to her highlights, and the closest she's got to a tennis racket in the last couple of years is watching the Australian Open—I'm sure you can guess the real answer!

PROLOGUE

'THIS is a nightmare!' Sucking in her breath, Annie closed her eyes as Melanie tugged at the back of her dress. 'But you get to wake up from nightmares.'

'It will be fine.' Melanie's voice was determinedly calm but it didn't fool Annie for a moment—especially when she dared to open her eyes again and stared at her reflection in the mirror. 'It will be fine...' Melanie said again, only with a dash less conviction—and with good reason: the fabulous mocha silk bridesmaid's gown that should slide over her stomach, creating a svelte sophisticated look, instead had a rather unfortunate ruching effect and Annie's usually rather insignificant bust was spilling out over the top of the empress line bodice.

'I look awful,' Annie wailed into the mirror. Her hair was everywhere, dark curls so wild they could have headed off on safari, blue eyes puffy from crying at the disaster of a dress that looked like it was going to burst open at the seams at any minute.

'You'll look great,' Melanie soothed her. 'Once your hair is done and everything and you're in high heels…you just need to loose a little bit of weight.'

'By Saturday!'

'Perhaps you could try a corset,' Melanie suggested. 'What was it like at the fitting last week?'

'Just a teeny bit tight—she was going to let it out a fraction over the bust and waist, but Jackie said there was no need, that if I hit the gym a bit harder it wouldn't be a problem.'

'And did you?' Melanie suddenly barked—all pretence at looking at the bright side dropping. 'Annie, I could hardly do it up. It's going to tear and Jackie's going to kill you when she finds out.'

There was nothing worse in a crisis than the

friend you've called on for support visibly crumbling. It was pathetic really, Annie tried to reason—the two of them both worked in the highly fraught, extremely busy emergency department of a large Melbourne hospital, dealt with life-and-death decisions each and every day and here they were, panicking, literally going to pieces, because she could barely get into her dress.

Oh, but it wasn't any dress—it was a bridesmaid's dress.

Worse—it was *Jackie's* bridesmaid's dress.

Jackie—her boss and friend, who had gone, in a matter of months, from deeply dedicated, fastidious consultant of her beloved emergency department to a self-absorbed, controlling bride-to-be.

And there were just six days to the wedding.

'My period is due.' Annie was really clinging at straws now. 'Maybe that's why it's so tight.'

'When?'

'Today, tomorrow…'

'Great.' Melanie was back in supportive mode now. 'It's probably a bit of fluid retention, and if you go on a crash diet and actually stick to it…well, you've seen those shows where they lose loads in the first week.'

'I'm not going on a crash diet.' Instantly Annie shook her head—a crash diet was the last thing someone with Annie's past should do, not that Melanie would know that. As close as they were, that murky bit of baggage had been thoroughly checked and deposited where it belonged—in the past. 'Anyway, they train for four hours a day…' Annie argued as Melanie looked at her watch. 'I'm supposed to be getting those nails put on this morning, so that I can be "used to them" by Saturday, then I'm on a late shift…' Annie shook her head—it was impossible, she had practise hair and make-up tomorrow evening, another late shift on Wednesday, the final rehearsal on Thursday night—oh, and a spray-on tan to squeeze in on Friday. There was absolutely no way she could fit in a triathlete's training schedule.

'Ring Jackie, then,' Melanie said. 'Ring Jackie and tell her that your dress doesn't fit.'

CHAPTER ONE

THE overhead lights in the observation ward were off as Annie Jameson swiped her ID card and raced in through the rear entrance of the accident and emergency department with a surprising ten minutes to spare before her late shift started.

Eight empty beds lay waiting to be filled—which was good news. The theory was that the obs ward should be cleared by midday—patients either discharged or transferred to a ward. But in practice that rarely happened: when a doctor saw an empty bed and his patient had been stuck in A and E for several hours too long, the obs ward invariably ended up becoming a mini high dependency unit—which the emergency department had to staff. Annie was one of the more senior nurses, which often meant that, rather than actually nursing, her time was taken up directing the never-ending flow of traffic in the department, finding beds, gurneys, staff and often transport.

'Hey, Annie,' came a few calls. Walking into the staffroom was as familiar and welcoming as walking into her own living room.

Midday was the busiest time—staff coming in for the late shift, doctors who were waiting for results and whoever had been allocated an early lunch—and seating was at premium. But, after placing her salad in the fridge and swigging on her water bottle, Annie saw that for once her favourite comfy chair was free and she collapsed with a loud groan and put her feet up on one of the coffee-tables.

'I'm exhausted,' she grumbled to her audience. 'It took an hour to get my nails done, then I had two painful hours at the gym, and…' Her voice sort of stopped, just for the teeniest, tiniest fraction of a second as she took in the unfamiliar face among her regular colleagues. 'I'm ready to drop. Is Jackie on today?'

'Is she ever?' Louise, a fellow associate charge nurse, rolled her eyes. There were two consultants—Marshall, who was winding down for retirement, and Jackie, who was winding up for a nervous breakdown. And currently *everyone* wanted to be working with Marshall. 'I'll be glad when this wedding is over,' Louise carried on. 'Everything, and I mean everything, ends up being about the wedding. I was setting up to put in a catheter and moaning that we were low on packs and somehow…'

Annie wasn't really listening. She looked, no doubt, as if she was listening, nodding in all the right places and adding little 'I know's' to the conversation. But instead her eyes were wandering, sort of casually drifting around the room, coming to rest on the clock so she could be sure she wouldn't be late for handover but sneaking a quick glimpse of the stranger who had caused her to falter.

Tall and dark, he was stretched out on a chair and he was stunning. Black hair, worn just a hint too long, framed a sculpted face, a full, very sulky mouth was moving to yawn and perhaps the reason she hadn't noticed him at first was because he didn't seem new.

New members of staff, whether porter or consultant, had that sort of anxious-to-fit-in look—and were either nodding furiously at the conversation or had their heads buried in a paper, trying to pretend they weren't there.

This delicious specimen, though, was scratching a rather unshaven chin and listening with vague interest to what everyone had to say.

And he'd caught her looking.

Slate-grey, almost black, and rather reprobate eyes held hers for just a second, that tiny second where you looked and he looked and it was just a tiny bit too long to be called polite, just that tiny fraction long enough to know that you were definitely female and he was definitely male—and both of you have noticed.

Her heart rate had only just recovered from her workout and now here it was edging over the 100 mark again.

Most of the staff in the room stood, draping stethoscopes round necks, checking paperwork or begging for a pen, while the early lunches remained sitting at the main table along with… Who was he?

'Hey, Iosef—you've got those blood gases to do.' Beth, one of her colleagues, addressed him.

'I'll be there soon.' There was just a smudge of an accent that Annie couldn't identify as Beth carried on talking.

'What time are you on until, then?'

'Ten,' came the surly reply.

Iosef.

Annie stayed with the pack as they all headed out to the floor and though two of Annie's most pressing questions had already been answered— his name was Iosef and he was here till ten—it just led to another. What sort of a name was Iosef?

'Gorgeous, isn't he?' Beth nudged Annie as

they made their way to Section A, which was the main hub of activity in Emergency.

'Who?' Annie attempted, but Beth just grinned.

'Don't even pretend you don't know who I'm talking about—the new senior registrar. Well, he's made it clear that he doesn't intend to stay a senior registrar for very long—he wants Marshall's position when he retires.'

'He's only just started here.'

'Oh, but he knows where he's finishing. I hope he gets it,' Beth added. 'He's just gorgeous—not that any of us mere mortals stand a chance. You know who he is, don't you?'

'You just said.' Annie frowned as they arrived at the nurses' station and waited for Cheryl, the charge nurse, to appear, ready to receive handover. 'He's the new senior registrar.'

'He's a Kolovsky!' Beth whispered, and Annie's jaw dropped. 'And not just a cousin five times removed—he's one of the sons.'

The Kolovsky family were Melbourne icons. Russian immigrants, Ivan Kolovsky along with his wife Nina had set up a fashion house years ago and now the House of Kolovsky had a reputation the world over for their stunning fashion designs and gorgeous fabrics. But here in Melbourne, where there was no royal family for the press to snap and a dearth of super-models and Hollywood film stars to photograph, the Kolovsky family added a necessary dash of international sizzle to the gossip columns—their inordinate wealth and lavish, jet-setting ways had them regularly hitting the headlines, and never more so than recently. The eldest son, Levander, a rake by anyone's standards, had recently fallen head over heels in love and got married, yet even though he and his wife had moved to the UK the press still followed them mercilessly—especially with the recent birth of their baby. And now Ivan Kolovsky, the founder and patriarch of the family, was rumoured to be on his deathbed—rumored because at every turn the Kolovskys' spin doctors issued denials. Barely a week went by without a mention of them in the press and on the news. As a lavish devotee of the glossies, Annie raked through the trashy part of her memory bank and came up with the necessary goods. Beth was telling the truth—one of the sons was a doctor.

'Wow.' Annie blinked at the rather drab surroundings, at the 24/7 organised chaos of a busy emergency department that just didn't somehow equate to the name Kolovsky. Despite the hour of the day a drunk was singing loudly in his cubicle and there was nothing glamorous about the pile of patients in the waiting room or the huddle of nurses awaiting handover—and she couldn't help but watch as he wandered through, a bag of ice in his hand, presumably on his way to do his blood gases.

'He's thoroughly spoken for,' Beth grumbled. 'You should see his girlfriend, Candy—she's absolutely stunning. Mind you, if he wants my opinion, she's just a touch old for him.'

'I'm sure he doesn't.'

'He might.' Beth grinned.

'You've seen her?'

'You will have, too—she's graced many a cover of *Vogue* in her day. She pops in now and then—all feverish and ravishing. Cow.' Beth pouted then gave a cheeky grin. 'Still, there's no law against looking.'

Handover took for ever—which it always did on Mondays. The department was heaving with the usual backlog of a heavy weekend, patients waiting in the corridors for the wards to empty out after the Monday morning ward round so they could be admitted.

'We've emptied the obs ward,' Cheryl said, 'but Jackie wants it to remain closed till six p.m.'

That was not an uncommon order on a Monday. The observation ward was supposed to be used only for emergency patients who would remain under the care of the emergency doctors—head injuries who needed twenty-four hours of regular observations before discharge or patients awaiting tendon repair—but all too often, when patients had already spent far too long on a hard gurney, it wound up filled with patients that belonged under other specialties, and this was the issue that they were trying to address.

'Right.' Cheryl peered down her list of nursing staff for the late shift. 'Beth, can you cover Resus? Annie, give her a hand if needed, and I want you take cubicles one through to five.'

'Sure.' Annie smiled, though she'd far rather be in Resus.

'Oh, I forgot to mention cubicle two's absolutely refusing to get undressed and be examined properly. We managed to get an ECG but that's it. Iosef said not to push it for now. He's waiting for a doctor to suture him. I've told the intern.'

'Who's the intern this afternoon?'

'George.' Cheryl rolled her eyes. 'We might actually get some work out of him this shift, given that Melanie's not on duty. Mind you, there's no real hurry to get cubicle two sutured— I'm pretty sure he's going to be admitted to Obs.'

Cubicle two turned out to be one Mickey Baker—a rather inebriated gentleman who'd provided the background music during handover, and was now snoring contentedly. And though in the real world it might make perfect sense to let him sleep off his excess, Annie needed to do a thorough set of neurological observations to set her own baseline in case he deteriorated during her shift.

'Afternoon, Mickey,' Annie called to her patient, and then called again. 'Mickey, can you open your eyes for me?' She watched as he struggled to do just that then thought better of it. 'Mickey, open your eyes, please, and tell me where you are.'

'Bloody hospital,' he growled, bloodshot eyes peeking open. 'Now, would you let me get some rest?'

'You know I can't do that, Mickey.' Annie smiled wryly, shining a torch in his eyes to check that his pupils were equal and responsive to light. 'Now squeeze my hands for me. Come on, squeeze them hard,' she insisted as Mickey reluctantly did as he was told. Clearly more than used to the drill, he lifted his legs in turn without being prompted as Annie checked off the boxes in her observation chart.

'Now can I rest?'

'For now,' Annie answered. 'Though I'll be back shortly to set up for the doctor to come in and suture you.'

'Any chance of something to eat, Annie?' Mickey asked, his eyes still closed. Annie couldn't help but smile. Mickey was one of their occasional regulars, coming in off the streets every few months. As well as getting his scalp sutured or his ulcers dressed or whatever it was that brought him in, he'd usually get a good feed and a much-needed bath and change of clothes before he went on his merry way. And though he hadn't been in for a few months now, that he remembered her name from last time brought an unseen smile to Annie's face.

'A lunch has been ordered for you—it should be here soon. After that we'll get you a bath—'

'I don't want a bath,' he snapped, rolling on his side. 'I just want something to eat.'

'Sure.' Annie nodded, but she gave a little unnoticed frown. Mickey was hiding something,
but till he'd sobered up and was a bit more co-
operative there really wasn't much that could be
done about it. 'You rest up till lunch comes and
whatever you do, don't get off the trolley. If you
need anything at all, just press the call bell.'

Her hand was up, about to swish the curtain
right back so Mickey could be easily watched,
when suddenly it was pulled back, making Annie
jump—and not just at the motion. Never had a
curtain opened on such a stunning cocktail of
sensations.

The breeze of the curtain was heavily laced
with the most potent male scent and close up
Iosef was even more divine. 'How is he?'

Annie wasn't exactly short, but he towered
over her. Even allowing for his rather more
senior status, he was superbly dressed. Black
trousers sat low on his slender hips, a thick white
cotton shirt with a thread count that was surely
in the millions set off a stunning gunmetal grey

tie that almost exactly matched his eyes. Though
Annie barely got a glimpse of them as he strode
past her and proceeded to take the blood-
pressure cuff off the wall and wrap it around a
grumbling Mickey's arm.

'Fine. I've just done his obs,' Annie said,
picking up the chart and offering it to him as he
pulled on his stethoscope. 'His blood
pressure's—'

'Shh…'

OK, a lot of people shushed others when they
were concentrating—no doubt, she did it herself
several times a day when she was trying to pick
up a difficult blood pressure or listening to a
chest—but it was more the way he'd shushed
her that had Annie's teeth grinding, the dismissive shake of his head, the brief wave of his free
hand as he shooed the obs chart away that had
her bristling.

'Good!' he said, more to himself than her,
taking off his stethoscope and wrapping it round
his neck before pinching Mickey's ear none too

gently. 'Afternoon, sir,' he called, and the old boy rolled over and requested, not too politely, that the doctor please just leave him alone. Annie spoke up again.

'I've just done his neuro obs.'

'Good.' He nodded, again completely ignoring the proffered chart, his findings clearly just to satisfy himself. 'Once I've sutured him, I want him moved to the observation ward.'

'I thought George was going to suture him.'

'He's my patient!' Iosef shrugged.

'Yes, but…' Annie started, unsure why a senior reg would choose to do the rather menial task—not that he was listening. Instead he was picking up the file and heading out through the curtains. 'Well, there's no rush, whoever stitches him. The obs ward is closed till six,' Annie called to his departing back. 'Jackie wants—'

'Jackie wants the beds used for emergency patients only—which Mr Baker is. Anyway, I want this cubicle cleared.'

'It just confuses things if we open it,' Annie protested. 'Other doctors see that it's open and—'

'Are you confused, Nurse?' he asked, halting her explanation in its tracks as she stared open-mouthed at possibly the rudest introduction to a colleague she'd ever experienced. 'Because if you *are* confused, I will explain things more simply: I want my patient in a bed, I want this cubicle to be utilised rather than providing a babysitting service because it's easier for the nurses to keep the obs ward closed. If you have a problem asserting yourself and telling doctors that they cannot use the emergency beds, send them my way and I will explain it to them.' He stalked out of the cubicle, leaving Annie to unwrap the blood-pressure cuff from the patient, her hand shaking with rage. Somehow he'd managed to condense more insults into a minute than most managed in a day. Her title was actually 'sister', though, given it sounded like a nun, she preferred Annie, but aside from that, assertion was as essential a qualification as a degree to make it in the emergency department, and for him to insinuate that she was lacking in that had Annie's blood boiling.

Still, there wasn't time to dwell on it now—the baby next door was due for his Ventolin and then she had to take one of her patients up to the ward—oh, and set up for Mickey to be sutured.

But in an almost reverse mirror image of moments ago, as Annie pulled open the curtains Iosef was just finishing up, giving the baby the last few puffs of his Ventolin through a spacer, though at least *this* time he did sign his name on the chart.

'Did you need something?' he asked, not even bothering to look up.

'What could I possibly need?' Annie gave a very twisted smile. 'You've clearly thought of everything!' And pursing her lips, she headed off to find Les, the porter, to come with her as they took her patient up to the ward.

She seethed every step of the way.

And not just on the first trip.

As her shift wore on, she felt more and more

useless beside the incredibly efficient, horribly arrogant and utterly loathsome Dr Kolovsky. It was actually closer to six by the time Mickey was eventually stitched, which made their earlier exchange rather pointless! Dr Fantastic set up for his own sutures and the happy laughter and chatter that came from behind the curtain as he joked with a now sober and much more compliant Mickey for some reason rankled Annie.

'There you go,' Annie heard him declare when she came in just as he was snipping the last stitch. 'As good as new.'

'I will be once I've had a bath.'

'That will be arranged—then I'll come and see you around there.'

'Thanks, Doc.'

Well, Mickey had changed his tune.

'Could you take him around now?' He didn't even look up. 'Jess has gone round to run his bath.'

'So soon after being sutured?' Annie checked.

'He wants a bath before he will allow me to examine him—I've spoken to Jess and she's to wait outside the bathroom door to listen out for him.'

Jess, one of the students, had indeed run Mickey a bath and he hopped off the trolley and into the bathroom, refusing all offers of assistance. As Jess hovered outside the bathroom door Annie started handover and catching sight of the scales, with Melanie's strict instructions still ringing in her ears, she unabashedly jumped on, moving the little weights to see where her weight was as she spoke to the student.

'He doesn't like being woken for his obs. He'll grumble like crazy but don't let him talk you out of it—he needs hourly neuro obs overnight. There's something else going on with him—normally he's not so bashful—but once he's had his bath he's agreed for Iosef to examine him. It will be interesting to see what's going on.'

'Any family that knows he's here?' Jess asked, and Annie shook her head as she gave a confused frown at the scales. 'That bad, huh?' the student asked sympathetically as Annie peered more closely at the scales.

'Actually, no!' Annie blew out a long breath. 'I weigh less than I thought I did.'

'Lucky you! That's good news, isn't it?'

'I guess,' Annie said, deciding it was too complicated to explain, but she stepped off and then back on again to make double sure the scales were right as she chatted on. 'Nope, no family— at least, none that he wants us to find out about. I've called the social work department and left a message for someone to come and have a chat with him in the morning and see if there's anything we can do for him, but I'm on tomorrow morning so I can chase it all up if…' Her voice trailed off as Iosef walked in, bored eyes rolling a fraction in greeting, but whereas only seconds ago she'd been standing on the scales, chatting and weighing herself without giving it a thought, Annie was now blushing self-consciously.

'Sorry to interrupt your weigh-in. I found Mickey Baker's ECG in my pocket. When you've got time, could you see that it's pasted to his notes? I'll be back once he's in bed.'

'Fine!' Annie bristled, as he tossed the beastly tracing on the desk and stalked off without a further word.

So he clearly thought her vain now as well as useless, Annie ranted to herself as she marched back round to the main area, thought she was a lightweight. She halted abruptly, and coolly eyed the chaos that reigned in cubicle two, the suture trolley he'd left behind was piled with dirty gloves and swabs. Her mood blackened further. He hadn't even disposed of his sharps and clearly he figured it was up to her to dispose of the rest of his mess, as well! Well, Annie decided furiously, tidying up. Whatever he thought of her he was about to find out just how assertive she could be, her grumbling stomach and a healthy dose of premenstrual tension not the ideal time, perhaps, for Iosef Kolovsky to suggest she was otherwise.

'Dr Kolovsky.' He was sitting at the nurses' station, writing his notes and looking as immaculate and groomed as he had at the start of the shift—unlike her. She was growing more and more disheveled. Her cheeks reddened with each and every trudge up to the ward, her hair wild from being pulled in exasperation at having spent the last few hours with a doctor who belonged in the middle of the previous century. 'Could I have a word, please?'

'Regarding?' He didn't even look up.

'Regarding the mess you just left in cubicle two.'

'What mess?' He glanced over at the empty cubicle then resumed writing. 'There is no mess.'

'Because I just cleaned it up.'

'Good.'

'I don't think you understand.' Annie cleared her throat. 'You can't just leave sharps and needles on a trolley—someone could hurt themselves!'

'I don't see the problem—you said yourself that you just cleaned them up!' He frowned, actually looked at her for the first time, his eyes holding hers, as if daring her to carry on, and for the first time Annie wondered if he was deliberately missing the point, especially when the edge of his lips twisted into just a hint of a smile. Well, if that was the case, she'd make things crystal clear.

'Yes, I cleaned them up,' Annie answered hotly, 'but for the last time. I don't know where you last worked, and you may think the only thing I'm capable of is running patients up to the ward or giving out bedpans, and if you choose to work that way, then go ahead and take the entire load, but don't ever compromise the safety of myself or my colleagues. If you choose to leave your mess for others to clean up, please, at least have the decency to at least clear away any sharps.'

'Sure.' He turned back to his writing, and heaped insult on insult by giving an utterly bored yawn as he effectively dismissed her, leaving her standing mouthing like a goldfish for a second before she turned on her heel.

'I'm sorry.' His apology stopped her in her tracks and slowly she turned around. 'I forgot. Normally,

I am meticulous about this sort of thing, but when I found his ECG I decided to bring it around—and the mess just slipped my mind.'

'Why didn't you just say so?' Annie frowned. 'You sat there, letting me rant.'

'You are very easy to goad…to wind up.' A glimmer of a smile twisted at the edge of his sulky mouth and he gave a small shrug as he returned to his notes. 'I couldn't resist. Again—I am sorry for the mess.'

'That's fine.' Disarmed by his niceness, she made the stupid mistake of giving him the benefit of the doubt, of thinking maybe she could have a normal conversation with him.

'What's going on with Mickey?'

'I don't know yet—I haven't examined him.'

'But did he say what—?'

'That's men's business,' he answered, effectively dismissing her.

'Fine,' Annie bristled. 'I'll just wait to read it in his notes.'

'Oh, and by the way, Nurse…' Her back stiffened as again he halted her, her rigid face turning as again he failed to use either her name or title. 'Your top…' He pointed to his own chest, made a tiny little gesture up and down with his finger before returning to his notes. Annie glanced down, aghast to see the top of her blouse gaping open. Worse, the ugliest, tattiest sports bra in the words was smiling up at her.

She refused to jump. If it had been any other of her colleagues they'd both have roared with laughter—but Iosef Kolovsky wasn't like anyone she'd ever worked with. So instead, ex-cruciatingly embarrassed, she walked as slowly and as calmly as she could towards the change rooms, holding her top together with one hand and grabbing a theatre top off the linen trolley. Only when she was safely inside and the door was closed did she let loose—a full afternoon and evening of humiliation and frustration hissing out in one single word.

'*Bastard!*'

Stunning to look at he might be, but he was

quite simply the most pompous, arrogant, loath-some person she had ever met. Why on earth hadn't Beth warned her about that?

Yet all her colleagues seemed utterly smitten with him—and most confusing to Annie as the shift wore on, the more horrible he was to her, the nicer he seemed to them. And the patients didn't seem to mind his rather austere bedside manner a single bit. He was so commanding, so utterly confident that it actually put them at ease. And he did listen to them, which was somewhat of a rarity among doctors—without interruption, too, that haughty face listening intently then quietly processing the information along with his findings and coming up with a swift diagno-sis and course of action.

And, who, Annie seethed late in the evening, among her colleagues could she complain to about a doctor that actually lightened their workload? He was completely autonomous, worked completely independently, and neither asked nor needed anyone's opinion or findings.

In fact, apart from the sharps incident, they really had little to say to each other—he just seemed to take every possible opportunity to wind her up.

Almost as if he'd singled her out to be horrible to.

'How's Mickey?' Annie asked Jess on the way to her break.

'Good.' Jess looked up from the desk. 'Iosef saw him and said to carry on with hourly neuro obs.'

'What was wrong?' Annie asked, reaching for his notes.

'He didn't say.'

He hadn't written it down either. Just a neat little entry giving the time of examination, and even though he didn't have to write it up straight away, Annie knew, just knew, that it had been a deliberate omission, that the meticulous Dr Kolovsky hadn't just forgotten…he was once again goading her.

Well, he could goad her all he liked, Annie decided, still seething at the end of her supper break as she headed back to the locker room.

Splashing her red cheeks with cold water, she dragged a comb through her wild hair.

He could wind her up as much as he jolly well liked and the more he did so, the more she'd smile!

'How are you going?' Realising she hadn't been in for a while and aware there were a couple of cardiac patients in Resus, Annie popped in to give Beth a hand. Given the serious nature of the patients in Resus, there were frequently controlled drugs to check, requiring two signatures, which the student who was helping out today wasn't qualified to check, and invariably there was something in a kidney dish awaiting a second pair of trained eyes. 'Need anything?'

'Everything is pretty much under control.' Beth popped her head around the drug cupboard. 'Iosef just checked the drugs with me.'

'Great!'

'Told you he was, didn't I?' Beth grinned. 'He's just so on the ball. Oh, actually, there is something you could do for me.'

'Sure!'

'Mr Evans, the anterior MI. Coronary Care just called down and they're ready for him. I don't want to send a student up with him in case he goes off *en route.*'

'No problem.'

Her face ached from smiling, her feet actually hurt from trudging up and down to the ward, and the absolutely last place Annie wanted to be at nine-thirty that night was pounding the treadmill at the gym, but Melanie had taken it upon herself to become her personal trainer, arriving at the end of Annie's shift, jangling her keys and waiting for her at the nurses' station, flirting blatantly with George the intern who was coming on duty for the night and chatting amicably to a smiling Iosef, who was bouncing a very grubby two-year-old on his knee.

'Here she is.' Melanie beamed. 'Ready for a workout?'

'As ready as I'll ever be,' Annie said, rolling her eyes.

'Thanks so much, Doctor!' The grubby two-year-old's mother blushed a little as she arrived to retrieve her son. 'It was really nice of you to hold him while I rang my husband.'

'No problem!' Iosef gave her a very nice smile.

'Have a good night, guys!' Melanie waved as they headed off.

'You too, Melanie,' Iosef answered.

As they headed out to the car park and off to the gym, it wasn't the prospect of a workout that had Annie's stomach sinking.

It was the lack of a goodbye from Iosef that had unsettled her.

Topped off by the smile he'd given Melanie as she'd waved back at him, that really irked.

The same smile she'd seen given to patients and colleagues.

The same smile that was noticeably absent around her.

CHAPTER TWO

IT WAS nice to be in Resus.

Annie loved the unpredictability and the rush of adrenaline that came from having to be constantly alert when nursing seriously ill patients—and there were certainly plenty of them this morning.

Both Beth and Melanie had been pulled from the cubicles to assist, and Cheryl, the charge nurse, was constantly popping in and out as no sooner had one patient been moved up to the ward than the paramedics wheeled in another, or a patient in the cubicles was deemed ill enough to transfer.

'Are you busy?' Iosef popped his head round the door and frowned at the activity.

'A bit.' Annie smiled, slightly taken aback that

he'd actually deigned to talk to her. 'Do you need a hand with anything?'

Silly question, she thought as he shook his head. 'I have an eighteen-month-old with an inhaled foreign body—it's a partial blockage.'

'Bring him over,' Annie said, ready to make room even if they didn't have any. A partial blockage to the airway could change in a matter of seconds but, despite the urgency of the situation, Iosef shook his head.

'I have rung the thoracic surgeons. They are in theatre, operating, but are going to send someone down. I think moving him over to Resus will only distress the child and that's the last thing I want.' With good reason, too, Annie thought as he placed the chest X-ray on the viewfinder and frowned at the precarious position of the foreign body. The object could move and the situation become potentially life threatening—everything possible needed to be done to keep the baby still and calm until the object could safely be removed by the surgeons. 'Get everything ready in case he fully obstructs. If he does, we'll bring him straight over…' Iosef continued picking up the telephone and barking his orders to the switchboard operator, peering at the X-ray again through narrowed eyes as he spoke at length to the thoracic surgeon while Annie quickly set up an emergency tray—a laryngoscope to allow clear vision of the larynx, McGill's forceps to pull out the foreign body—and pulled in a trolley ready for the toddler should they need it. 'I am going to take him straight up to Theatre—they're expecting him now. He can sit on Mum's knee on a wheelchair. But I want a porter to push the trolley and resus equipment should I need it on the way. I'll also need a nurse to come.'

'Fine.' Annie nodded, pressing an intercom button and summoning the porter then loading up the trolley with the equipment she had gathered. 'I'll just let Cheryl know that I'm—'

'Beth…' Ignoring Annie, Iosef called out to her colleague as she raced past. 'I want you to come up to Theatre with me.'

Surplus to requirements again.

Though it made sense. After all, yesterday when Beth had been in charge of Resus it had been she herself racing around the hospital, and Beth had no doubt already had contact with the child out in the cubicles, but it was the way Iosef again dismissed her that irked Annie.

Not that there was time to dwell on it.

Space needed to be cleared in Resus and after a rather terse conversation with ICU, Annie dispatched Melanie to take up a patient with a severe head injury who had commandeered most of the morning and now that her chest-pain patient was more settled, a semblance of order was finally taking shape.

For about ten seconds.

'Fifty-seven-year-old male....' Geoff, the paramedic, gave a running handover as they rolled the stretcher along the polished floor. 'Liver cancer with secondary mets. Started seizing at home, private nurse present, she's just giving details at Reception. The wife's following in a car. He was given rectal diazepam but…' He didn't need to elaborate as the frail body on the stretcher started convulsing again, the grey tinge to his face becoming more deeply cyanosed as the paramedic wrestled with the straps and the patient was lifted over.

Annie transferred the portable oxygen to the wall outlet and was attaching monitors as Jackie, seeing what was going on, kicked over the drug trolley and started pulling up drugs. 'Thanks, guys,' Jackie said as the paramedics, always happy to help out, held a jerking arm still while she administered anti-seizure medication.

They continued to relay the story. 'He's supposed to have been transferred to a palliative care ward of a private hospital, but the wife wants him at home. He's been having prolonged seizures but they normally respond to the diazepam. This one went on for ages and the wife wanted him bought in.'

'We need a full history,' Annie called after Geoff, who was heading to register the patient at

Reception. 'Tell whoever's on Reception to drop everything, that we need it urgently. Do you want an anaesthetist?' she asked Jackie, trying to suction the patient with one hand and pull the phone out of her apron with the other.

'Let's get the history first,' Jackie said. 'I don't want to intubate him if it turns out he's not for resuscitation.'

'One other thing.' Eric, the second paramedic, was sweating with the exertion of holding the arm still as Jackie shot in more drugs. 'The wife says that his son's a doctor here. This is Ivan Kolovsky…you know, the fashion designer?'

Jackie's eyes met Annie's just as Beth breezed in.

'Need a hand?'

'Where's Iosef?' Jackie asked, adding more medication to an IV flask as Annie suctioned Ivan's airway. His eyes had rolled back in his head, his body exhausted from seizing for so long.

'On his way. He was just talking to the thoracics. Why?'

'Meet Mr Kolovsky!' Jackie said with a dry

edge. 'Annie, you go and tell Iosef what's happening—preferably before he walks in here. Beth—give me a hand.'

Clearly Iosef hadn't hung around to make small talk with the thoracics because as Annie sped out of Emergency, hoping to meet him in the corridor and forewarn him, they practically collided at the glass automatic doors.

'Iosef…' Annie called as he marched past without even a cursory glance. 'Can I have a word?'

'I'm busy.' He didn't even turn his head to call it over his shoulder.

'I need to talk to you!' she snapped loudly, angry that he made everything so difficult, angry that he was so rude, and nervous at what she had to tell him!

'Well, make it quick. I have a lot of work.'

He just stood there—stood there right in the middle of the corridor, didn't move near a wall, didn't duck into the quieter reception area, didn't do a single thing to make it easier—just tapped his well-shod foot impatiently as Annie took a deep breath. 'Could we go somewhere a bit more private?'

'Why?' He frowned.

'Because I need to discuss a patient with you.' Her cheeks were burning under his scrutiny and out of the corner of her eye and behind his shoulder she could see a rather glamorous mob spilling into Reception, who had to be related to him! 'And I don't think the corridor's a very appropriate place.'

He gave her a thoroughly bored, thoroughly superior look as if to say there was nothing she could possibly tell him that he didn't already know, but at least he did take a few sideways steps into the IV cupboard and stood there shrugged up against the wall as Annie closed the door and flicked on the light.

'Your father's just been brought in.' Direct and straight to the point she gave him the news and equally as direct and straight to the point he asked her a question.

'Is he dead?'

'No, but he's convulsing and we're having a lot of trouble stopping that.' She watched his face for a reaction, but it was utterly unreadable, and in all her years of nursing, all the times she'd broken bad news or difficult news or *any* sort of news, never, not even once, had anyone shown so little response—not a single flick of his eyes, not one tense swallow. Annie could only liken it to dashing to the shops at six p.m. and finding a 'Closed' sign on the door, not a 'Back in five' sign, not even 'Back tomorrow'. Peering into the windows of his soul, all she could see was nothing, just nothing, as if every shelf had been stripped bare.

'Thank you.'

He didn't ask for more information, didn't ask anything of her, just turned and opened the door and headed for Resus. Annie followed him, the rather breathless anaesthetist arriving a second after them, but Iosef took immediate control.

'He is not to be intubated. He is a terminal patient and for palliative care only.'

'We're just waiting on his notes.'

'His notes are at the private hospital,' Iosef responded, picking up a wall phone and tapping in a number. 'I will get his oncologist to speak with you now.'

'Thanks.' Jackie gave a grateful nod. It was excruciatingly hard dealing with a colleague's relative, especially one so sick, and it would be far easier to go through his history and prognosis with his doctor rather than his son.

'He's stopped seizing,' Annie said.

The tiny spasms in his hands, the flickering of his eyelids, had ceased now and Ivan fell into a heavy post-ictal state, his exhausted body dragging in air.

Jackie spoke to Iosef. 'His stats are dire and his respiration rate is dangerously low.'

'I can see that.' He flicked a light in his father's eyes, examining him carefully, and it could have been any other patient except that he spoke to the unconscious man in Russian, checking his reflexes before replacing the blanket. The only time his shoulders tensed, the only time she saw his jaw clench was when the family was ushered in, the receptionist apologetically introducing Nina Kolovsky whose loud, throaty sobs filled the room.

'I asked if she'd wait in the interview room,' Kath, the receptionist, said to Jackie as Nina's knees buckled at the sight of her husband. 'She insisted that she be with him.'

'That's fine, Kath,' Iosef said, then spoke in Russian to his mother, abrupt words that halted her tears but had her arguing loudly with him. But Iosef wasn't having any of it, taking his mother firmly by the elbow and leading her outside as Jackie spoke at length on the phone to the oncologist across the city before hanging up.

'He's not for intubation or resuscitation,' Jackie relayed. 'Iosef has been trying to get Nina to have him admitted to a palliative care ward, but so far she's demanding that he be nursed at home. The ward here is more than happy to take him as, frankly, I think he's way too ill to be transferred—let's wait and see what Iosef has to say.'

Not very much.

After just a few moments he returned, his face a touch grey now but his voice extremely steady when he spoke.

'My mother saw something on the news last night about a treatment.' He shook his head at the hopelessness of it all. 'She refuses to accept that he is dying—even with round-the-clock nursing and his doctor coming in, she panics all the time. She does not want him to be admitted to the private hospital, but he cannot stay at home like this.'

'I don't think he's well enough to be transferred anyway,' Jackie said softly. 'Iosef, would you like to come to my office? We can—'

'That will not be necessary.' Again he shook his head, rubbed the top of his forehead with his index finger for a few seconds as he stared at this father, and for no apparent reason Annie felt a well of tears in her eyes, knew, *knew* that despite his cool demeanour, despite the fact he appeared supremely in control, detached even—somewhere deep inside this had to hurt. 'I will ring his hospital and have him admitted to their medical ward. I should be able to get her to agree to that and perhaps then we can discuss getting him transferred to the palliative care ward.'

'Iosef,' Jackie said slowly, 'I've told you—he's not well enough to go in an ambulance.'

'I am well aware of that.' Grey eyes held Jackie's. 'I am also aware of the circus this will become once the media find out that he has been admitted. The private hospital is better equipped to deal with that. I also know my family, Jackie, and this is the only way I can think of to get my father the care he needs at this late stage. So give me whatever it is I need to sign and I will escort him in the ambulance.'

Which didn't leave much room for manoeuvre.

Still, by the time the ambulance arrived, it felt like every Russian living in Melbourne had trooped through Resus to pay their respects. Ivan Kolovsky was propped up on pillows, sipping lukewarm tea through a straw and cursing in Russian as Annie did his final set of obs before he headed off to the private hospital.

'What's he saying?'

'You don't want to know.' Iosef gave a dry smile.

'Tell me.' Annie grinned. 'I won't be shocked.'

'Oh, you would…' His eyes actually held hers, beautiful, beautiful grey eyes that had a tiny swirl of navy around the outer rim of his iris, and she was grateful for what came next, grateful that what he said could allow for the pink flush that came to her cheeks as she held his gaze. 'No one can insult like a Russian.'

'I'd already worked that one out!' Annie retorted, and for the first time they actually shared a smile.

Even though the department was busy, it felt empty when Ivan went—or rather when Iosef went with him. Even though every bed in Resus was full, for Annie it felt…

Empty.

As if she'd walked into the lounge and watched five minutes of the most amazing film only for the power to cut, leaving her feeling like she was missing the most vital piece of the picture. So, when her shift was over, she was unusually reluctant to leave, standing idly flicking through a magazine and chatting to Jackie.

'It must be hard on him.' Turning the pages, Annie paused and stared at a very grainy *exclusive* photo of Levander Kolovsky's new baby which had clearly been taken through a very long lens. 'I mean, imagine having your father so sick and having to worry about the press getting hold of it.'

'We've already had a load of enquiries from the press.' Jackie yawned, stretching and moaning in a chair at the nurses' station and, annoyingly for Annie, again changing the subject back to her wedding.

'I've had the worst day! I told you about my cousins, didn't I?'

'You did,' Annie sighed.

'How they could have left it till now to book a flight, I simply don't know…' Annie felt her heart skip a beat as Iosef returned, swishing through the swing doors and looking so cranky and exhausted and gorgeous she had to stop herself from jumping up and greeting him, her mind flitting in and out of the conversation as Jackie droned on and on about her blessed wedding preparations! 'I mean, they've known for months when the wedding is. Well, if they think I'm going to sit on the computer tonight, trying to find the cheapest one left, they can jolly well think again—I've got enough on my plate. The florist is— Oh, hi, Iosef, how is he doing?'

'Cantankerous!' He gave a tight smile. 'But yet again he surprises us all. He wants to be discharged, they're trying to persuade him to stay till the morning. How are things here?'

'All yours! I'll be back at midnight.' Jackie rolled her eyes and handed him a stack of pagers. 'Can you make sure you're here at eight sharp tomorrow morning? I've got to get to the caterers.'

'Of course.' Iosef nodded.

'Did you try that wine?'

'Sorry…' Annie caught his frown, watched,

annoyed at Jackie, as Iosef clearly had to drag his mind back to her strange train of thought.

'The one I told you about. You know I think it might just be a touch too sweet. I mean, when I tasted it I thought it was fabulous but now I'm starting to worry that it might be a bit overpowering.'

'It's great!' For the second time that day he caught Annie's eyes, even gave a thin smile as she winced in apology for her colleague. 'You've made an excellent choice.'

'Really?' Jacked asked earnestly, but didn't wait for an answer, and Annie let out a long breath as she hurried off. They stood in awkward silence for a very long minute, until finally, bravely, Annie broke it.

'She's really not like that normally.'

'It's fine.'

'No, it's not,' Annie contradicted him. 'That was horribly insensitive.'

And at that point she expected him to turn his back—terminate the conversation as he always did, be the Iosef he always was with her. But maybe he was tired, or maybe he just needed to talk. She couldn't really identify it, couldn't really, no matter how she replayed it later that night, define the moment, define how it felt, when, for the first time, he not only prolonged a conversation with her but actually let her glimpse a little piece of him.

Actually, called her by her name.

'I grew up with insensitive, Annie. Really, I don't need Jackie feigning concern.'

'Still…'

'Honestly—it's not a problem.'

'Do you want a coffee?' Annie offered, though she'd sworn she never would, but he looked so tired and his mind must surely be all over the place—it seemed the right thing to do. 'I can grab you one before I go.'

He pulled a face. 'No, thanks. I've had about twenty today.'

'Fine…' she hitched her bag higher on her shoulder before she turned to go. 'I am sorry, today must have been…' She struggled for the appropriate word and settled for the only one she could think of. 'Hard.'

'You know, there is something you could do for me.' He wasn't looking at her, instead he was looking at her bag—or rather the massive sun-dried tomato and herb flavoured pretzel peeking out of it, which she'd bought in a moment of weakness. 'I'm starving and I don't have any change for the machine.'

'Enjoy…' Annie grinned, handing the shiny packet over.

'You don't mind?'

'Not at all,' Anne said, and patted her stomach. 'In fact, you're actually doing me a favour.'

CHAPTER THREE

ONE more day… Increasing the speed and elevation on the treadmill, Annie took a slug of water from her bottle and nearly lost her footing as she pounded the rubber.

Every morning she'd resisted the overwhelming temptation to hit the snooze button. As an added incentive she'd hung the beastly dress on her curtain rail, and it had served its purpose—the dark slender silhouette the first thing she peered at in the morning.

And with any luck it would have had some effect because tomorrow was Friday.

One more day of waking at the crack of dawn and joining the strange specimens of human life who actually seemed to enjoy being here.

She'd been one of them once.

Six a.m. wasn't the best time for introspection perhaps, but walking and not moving was doing her head in, and watching the swimmers slicing the water below wasn't exactly riveting viewing.

She'd been scared when Melanie had suggested that she crash-diet.

Scared because she'd been there and done that once before.

She didn't need Melanie to tell her the calorie content of anything because she knew it all already—knew more than Melanie or anyone should ever know about how to lose weight. Like the treadmill she was pounding now, Annie remembered the hamster wheel she'd once climbed on, thriving on the usually absent approval from her mother as she'd whittled away her puppy fat, frantically chasing two sisters who had always been thinner, prettier, cleverer, always that bit ahead, forcing herself ever on as the approval from her mother had changed to concern, as the goalposts had kept shifting, until her only focus had been to keep going.

Thankfully she'd jumped off.

Had seen the error of her ways before things had become too dangerous, but she'd glimpsed the dark side of the street and had sworn she'd never go back there. Still, she was glad that she had done this one week, glad because it had shown her that she was really free of it, that once the wedding was over, normal services would resume. Just the rehearsal to get through tonight and the tan tomorrow and then she'd try on her dress and if it didn't fit, well, she'd tried. Annie knew at that point she should probably have been motivated enough to up the elevation a touch more, but she was almost beyond caring, so instead she pressed the 'cool down' button, gulping water as the treadmill gradually wound its way down. Walking as she stared out of the gym window at the pool complex down below and idly watching as someone in the fast lane came in so fast, that for a second Annie thought he was going to hit the wall, that he wasn't going to turn in time. Instead he had finished, strong arms heaving his body out of the water, and for the second time that morning Annie lost her footing on the treadmill.

Watching the swimmers was actually riveting viewing after all—well, one swimmer in particular!

It was him.

And whoever had suggested that imagining people who intimidated you without their clothes on to make things easier had clearly never seen Iosef Kolovsky with practically nothing on.

His body was divine. Even from this distance, Annie could see his body was superbly toned, wide shoulders tapering down to a very flat stomach. Annie swallowed as he strode across the floor and came delightfully into better focus. His bathers, heavy with water, were down just low enough on his hips to allow the viewer a glimpse of a delicious line of hair, a decadent arrow that pointed downwards , but as she rather reluctantly dragged her eyes upwards Annie was mortified to find him staring up at her, realising then that the treadmill was at a complete standstill. That she'd absolutely, one hundred per cent certainly been caught—not just staring but drooling!

So she'd looked at him, Annie tried to reason with herself, but even the cold jets of the shower couldn't soothe the blush that had swept over her. If it had been anyone else from work she'd have looked over when she noticed them but she'd have waved if they'd seen her, Annie conceded. She certainly wouldn't have stood transfixed on a motionless treadmill, gawping. And all too soon she'd have to face him—in fact, if she didn't step on it she'd be late for work.

What was it with Iosef Kolovsky?

Yes, he was good-looking and, yes, he had a fabulous body, but he was also arrogant, opinionated and downright rude—at least he was with her Annie fumed as, shivering now, she turned off the shower and grabbed her towel from the peg.

She'd been staring daggers at him, Annie

decided hopefully, pulling her stuff out of her locker, or perhaps she could pretend that she needed glasses and had been squinting, trying to make out if she knew him. All these thoughts were being processed as she tried to wrestle a damp body into a pair of knickers. She paused as she straightened up, the pale heel of a foot jutting out from under one of the shower doors catching her eye. From its position it was clear that whoever the foot belonged to was lying on the floor.

'Hello,' she called out. 'Are you OK?'

No response.

Annie grabbed up her towel, wrapping it around her as she crossed back over to the showers. She banged on the door with one hand, trying to rouse whoever the unfortunate person was, while with the other she palpated the foot, relieved to feel a pulse but knowing that her banging wasn't going to rouse whoever was in there. The shower was running and if blasts of cold water weren't having an effect then her banging wasn't going to do anything.

The woman could be drowning on the other side of the door, Annie realised with horror, lying face down in a pool of water…

She needed help!

Urgently!

Only this wasn't Emergency, where she could press a bell and summon a team. Running back, Annie grabbed a coin out of her purse, spilling most of its contents on the floor. Then she quickly yanked open the changing-room door and called out for assistance, startling a young guy who was walking past the door towards the gym, earphones in place and bag over his shoulder. Clearly not expecting a dripping wet woman, wrapped in a towel and looking frantic, jumping out at him on his way to his morning workout.

'Go to the desk and tell them we need an ambulance.' Annie's voice was slightly breathless but clear. 'Tell them there's a woman collapsed and unconscious in the shower and to send someone up to help with the door.' She hadn't finished talking before the young man dropped his bag and fled for the reception area.

Knowing that help was on the way allowed her to breathe just a touch easier, and back at the shower cubicle she attempted to use the coin she'd grabbed from her purse to turn the lock from the outside, a trick she'd used many times before. Collapsed patients in showers and toilets were not an unknown predicament in Emergency but as Annie freed the lock and pushed on the door, she realised with a sinking feeling that the worst possible scenario had transpired. The collapsed body in the confined space was wedging the door closed so forcing the door would be useless and could only injure the patient further. She didn't even turn her head as the changing-room door slammed open and footsteps raced to join her.

'Don't,' Annie ordered as a rather burly personal trainer faced the door shoulder on. 'It's jammed by the patient.'

'I'll ring Maintenance, get them to take it off,' he offered.

But Annie wasn't listening. Instead she was eyeing the impossibly small gap between the shower wall and the ceiling and wishing she'd been on her diet for more than four days!

'What's the story?'

She'd know that voice anywhere, and even though to that point she'd barely given a thought to her lack of attire, suddenly Annie was acutely aware that she was dressed in little more than a towel.

He didn't even wait her response, just assessed the situation in seconds.

'You're the only one small enough.'

The personal trainer went to crouch, his palms pleated together to make a step, but Iosef wasn't wasting a second, his hands gripping her waist and hoisting her up to the wall where she clung none too elegantly as he let go and placed her waving feet on his shoulders. Thank the Lord she'd at least had time to put on knickers.

'Can you see anything?' he demanded impatiently, but the gap was too high and too narrow and until she was on the other side there would be nothing to report.

He was so tall that from her position, standing on his shoulders, it wasn't that far a stretch to get her right leg over the partition and squeeze through the gap. She looked down to the shower floor below, ignoring his impatient questions as she chose a piece of floor space where she could safely drop. It was not a clear drop, though, as she grazed her left leg on the partition and gave a rather large yelp.

'What's happening?' Iosef called.

'I just caught my leg!' Annie snarled through gritted teeth.

'I meant with the patient.'

She was a large lady, half sitting, half lying against the opposite partition wall, her shoulders wedging the door awkwardly, and Annie noted with disquiet the awkward position of her head was actually half blocking her airway.

'Completely unresponsive, no signs of injury' Annie called. 'Laboured resps. I'm going to have to position her, she's blocking her airway.'

'Can you lay her down?'

The door's going to have to come off! Unless…'

'Unless what?' he barked.

'I might be able to shift her around enough to get the door open, but she could have a neck injury.'

'She could well be a corpse with a neck injury if we don't get to her soon,' Iosef pointed out—and in this instance he was right. Although a patient generally shouldn't be moved, her position was actually life-threatening and though Annie would do all she could to support her alignment, she had no choice but to move her. She raised the woman's head a fraction and her breathing was instantly less noisy and laboured. 'I'm throwing a towel over to you—use that under her arms so you can get a grip. Does she have a medic alert bracelet or anything?'

Annie rolled her eyes. 'I think I might have managed to mention it if I'd seen one.'

'No time for sarcasm, Nurse!' She could almost

see his smile as he delivered his rebuke, but rather than respond she got on with the job in hand.

'Here.' She pulled off a rubber bracelet with a key on it from around the unconscious woman's wrist and threw it under the door.

'That's not an alert—' Iosef started then stopped, telling the trainer to go to the locker and search it.

'Could you throw a couple more towels?' Annie called, and even if Iosef didn't give a damn as to whether or not the patient was naked, as a few towels were thrown over, Annie knew that no matter how dire the situation she'd want whoever found her to take a couple of seconds to preserve her dignity.

On the other side of the door she could hear Iosef barking orders to her, but Annie wasn't actually listening—there was no effective advice that could be offered from someone who hadn't seen and assessed the situation. The best she could do now was rely on her own instinct.

God, she was heavy. The woman's dead

weight and the slippery tiles combined to make the task exhausting, but finally Annie managed to angle her enough that the limp body was leaning against her and, doing as Iosef had said, she placed a towel under the woman's armpits and gripped her as she leant backwards. She watched with a mixture of frustration and relief as the door opened a few inches, allowing Iosef to look inside.

Why did he have to look so fabulous?

Of course, in theory it shouldn't have mattered a jot what the doctor on the other side looked like, but just as she had preserved her patient's dignity, it would have been nice to preserve her own. But, of course, Dr Perfect looked impeccable while she lay sprawled, drenched and positively beetroot with exertion on the floor.

'Just a few inches more—come on, Annie,' Iosef ordered.

Which was fine for him to say, Annie thought, grunting with the exertion of it all.

She hadn't actually seen him when he'd first

burst into the changing room; her mind so busy with the task in hand, she'd more heard him, been aware of him—only now she could see him and it was impossible not to notice the contrast between them. A fraction of a second to take in his immaculate appearance. His hair was wet but, unlike Annie's, it was neatly combed backwards, utterly unruffled he stood resplendent in a suit. The only ungroomed part of him was that he hadn't yet shaved, but then again, her mind quickly processed, in the short time she'd known him he'd always had that smudge of designer stubble on his strong jaw.

'Where is she bleeding?' he asked, seeing the reddish tint to the water and running his hands through the woman's hair.

'That's mine!' Annie said tightly, neither expecting nor receiving a shred of sympathy.

'It could be cardiac.' He was crouching down, feeling a carotid pulse with one hand and lifting the unfortunate woman's eyelids with the other, his scent heavy in the confined space.

'Hypoglycaemia,' Iosef said, more to himself than her, 'or stroke.'

He was working his hands down her body, then pulled out a pen and scraped the soles of her feet to check the woman's reflexes, breathing a sigh of relief as the response was correct, her big toes pointing downwards. Had they lifted, for example, it might have indicated a cerebral problem. His expensive pen was, for now, Iosef's only diagnostic tool, and he continued to wield it without pause, rolling it against the bed of her fingernails to check her response to pain.

'How long for the ambulance?'

'Soon,' Annie said helplessly. 'It seems like ages but it's only probably been—'

'I've got her bag.' Even the personal trainer was breathless. 'It was one of the lockers down by the pool,' he explained, but Iosef wasn't listening. He was tipping out the contents like a kid with his stocking on Christmas morning. The riddle was solved before the contents had even hit the wet floor, a small diabetic kit drawing their eyes. Without a beat of hesitation both set to work, Annie pricking the woman's finger and placing a drop of blood on the dextrose strip as Iosef pulled out a glycogen injection and snapped it open.

'Naught point two,' Annie called and within seconds he had delivered the vital injection.

The paramedics arrived moments later.

'Hypoglycaemic!' Iosef called. 'She hasn't got a scrap of glucose in her. I want IV dextrose!' Even though the woman had been given a glucose injection, it had been given into the muscles and would take a longer to work than intravenously—and given the current state of her sugar level, time was of the essence, dextrose urgently needed to prevent brain damage. Iosef didn't introduce himself as a doctor as he barked his orders, and whether or not the paramedics recognised him from emergency was almost im-material—he was so commanding, so utterly in control of the situation there could be absolutely no question he knew what he was doing.

Or maybe it was that they knew Annie!

Oh, the morning was just getting better and better.

One of the paramedics slipped an oxygen mask on the patient while the other pulled up the drug, both managing to have a cheeky laugh at Annie's predicament.

'You just can't keep out of trouble, can you, Annie?' Eric laughed.

Seemingly not as, standing on legs that were rather shaky, one hand holding the vital towel, she finally picked her way out of the tiny cubicle. But instead of immediately heading for her clothes, she lingered, pulling the blanket off the stretcher and trying from the doorway to drape her patient. Staying to watch for just a moment more—seeing a patient in a hypoglycaemic coma being given IV dextrose was just one of those things that as a nurse it was nice to see—hopefully a rapid, happy outcome to a medical emergency.

Iosef had already inserted a bung before the solution had been pulled up—a large syringe was required and, given the thick, sticky nature of the solution, it took a while to draw it through the needle. She watched as Iosef picked up a wallet from the floor and pulled out a driver's licence before delivering the vital solution. As a nurse Annie knew how important it was to use a patient's name, particularly when they came to. Wow, he was impressive.

Annie couldn't help but smile as the instant miracle occurred.

'It's OK, Grace.' Iosef's voice was calm and re-assuring as his patient's eyes flickered open, flaccid limbs suddenly jerking into motion, a look of confusion on her face as she struggled to sit up and orientate herself. 'Your blood sugar was low but it's OK now. Just lie back down…' A look of horror darted across Grace's face as she started to process her surroundings as her hands flailed to cover herself, but still he reassured her. 'You're fine, you're covered. I'm a doctor and there are paramedics here. In a moment we're going to move you onto a stretcher.'

And a nurse, Annie thought, a flash of something she couldn't quite identify coursing through her as with a shrug she sorted out her clothes and slipped unnoticed into one of the cubicles, wondering why she let him bother her so.

As an emergency nurse, recognition and appreciation was always lacking—not just from patients, from colleagues too sometimes. But something, something about Iosef's dismissal of her efforts, her everything, irked her. 'I don't need to go to hospital,' Grace attempted, but Iosef was having none of it.

'You're going.'

She was. In no time the paramedics had her on a stretcher and on her way, shouting a quick goodbye to Annie as she pulled on the top of her uniform behind the cubicle door.

'See you guys. Thanks!' Annie called cheerfully, pressing the towel to her shin to stop the blood flow, feeling stupid for the tears that were filling her eyes because her leg hurt like hell.

It was pure adrenaline, Annie told herself,

sticking on a few plasters retrieved from the bottom of her bag. Then, having pulled on navy stockings and a skirt, she hobbled out of the cubicle to the mirror. The previously deserted changing room was fit to bursting now as it filled with the backlog the emergency had created. Dragging a comb through her hair, she saw her red nose and the overflowing pool of tears in her eyes and attempted a sniff to hold them back.

It was the excitement of the morning catching up with her and the fact she'd barely eaten a thing since Monday. Tears were really threatening now and, angry with herself, Annie held them back. She slung her bag over her shoulder and hobbled out of the gym. It was nerves about the wedding perhaps, Annie explained to herself, and her now very sore leg wasn't helping much. Taking a gulp from her water bottle, Annie willed herself calm before starting the car engine and heading for work.

She certainly wasn't upset because Iosef Kolovsky hadn't even bothered to say goodbye.

CHAPTER FOUR

'IT's bad enough you're late, but you have the nerve to swan in here with a bacon sandwich and a take-out coffee.' Walking into the staffroom to dump her bag, Annie jumped as she unwittingly walked into the midst of two senior doctors rowing. Jackie was apoplectic, her hand shaking as she ripped off her white coat and sensible shoes, her eyes bulging with rage as she changed into a pair of killer stilettos and spritzed herself with deodorant. 'You know there has to be a senior doctor here at all times. Marshall's working tonight and you know I've got to see the florist and caterers this morning…' On and on she went as Iosef just stood there, leaning against the lockers, lazily eating his sandwich, as Jackie raged on.

Lazily leaning against Annie's locker!

'Excuse me,' she mumbled to him when Jackie paused for breath.

'Have you any idea how hard it is to arrange a wedding *and* work up to the last minute? All I asked is that you get here at eight sharp this once.' He wasn't leaning against the lockers now—in fact, he was heading for the door, turning his back on the consultant. Enraged, she called him back.

'I haven't finished yet, Dr Kolovsky.'

'I've heard enough,' he called over his shoulder as he opened the door, and Jackie literally froze on the spot. Iosef was possibly the first person to ever really stand up to her when she was in one of her moods, but Iosef hadn't actually finished yet. Before walking out, he turned and looked at her. 'In fact, to be totally honest, I think everyone's heard enough about your wedding! Now, if you'll excuse me, I've got patients to attend to.'

The silence that followed the slam of the door

was excruciating. Jackie's cheeks flushed with rage and embarrassment and Annie wished a trapdoor would magically open beneath her, especially when anxious eyes met hers.

'Is that true?' Jackie's voice was wobbly, the efficient controlled consultant gone as she ran a shaking hand through her newly highlighted hair. 'I mean, I might have gone on a bit…' Her voice trailed off, her eyes darting as no doubt she relived the past few weeks through her colleagues' and family's eyes. 'Did he mean that?'

'He's just upset,' Annie attempted. 'A woman collapsed at the gym this morning.'

'At the gym.' Jackie frowned.

'In the shower next to me. Iosef was there, swimming. He must have heard the commotion and stepped into help. She was wedged behind a door—it took for ever to get her out.'

'That's why he was late?'

Annie nodded. 'Mind you, given the circumstances, I guess stopping at the canteen for a dose of bacon and coffee was pushing it a bit.'

'He's supposed to be on a day off,' Jackie said through pale lips. 'He's covering for me—I've got back-to-back clinics this morning as well as covering Emergency. Hell, I'd have stopped for something to eat—he's not going to get a chance all day. I've been a real pain, haven't I?'

'You've been like any excited bride,' Annie attempted, 'just a bit…'

'I've been awful,' Jackie moaned. 'You know, when Jeremy asked me, I wanted something quick and easy. I mean, I'm forty-two—who the hell wants a big white wedding at forty-two?'

'You do.' Annie smiled softly, taking her friend's hand and welcoming her back, even teasing her as she would have in another life— one before the engagement. 'You want the church and the flowers and the bridesmaids all colour co-ordinated and all the trimmings that go with it. And that's fine, Jackie. You've waited a long time and you want your day to be perfect.'

'I'm just so worried that something will go wrong if I don't stay on top of everything.'

'Nothing's going to go wrong,' Annie assured her. 'It's going to be wonderful. Now, you'd better get going. I'll see you tonight at the rehearsal.'

There was a whole day to get through before then, though, and her leg was really starting to hurt. Heading over to the nurses' station, Annie offered her apologies to Cheryl but she waved them away.

'Iosef told us what happened. You're to register and pop into cubicle two.'

'What?'

'He said you gashed your leg.'

'It's just a cut, there's no need—'

'I wouldn't argue with Iosef if I were you,' Cheryl sighed. 'He's like a thundercloud this morning. He's only been here ten minutes and he's upsetting everyone. If I were you, I'd just go and register.'

Sitting on the chair in cubicle two, Annie dabbed at the cut with some antiseptic, dreading him coming in and pathetically grateful that, thanks to Jackie's unwavering schedule, she'd had her legs waxed yesterday. Not that he'd care. As he swept in to the cubicle he barely even looked at her as he instructed her to climb up on the trolley.

'I don't need to lie on the trolley.'

'I would rather you did.' He stood his ground. 'Because I'd rather not bend.'

God, he was loathsome. Annie prickled as she climbed up onto the trolley and sat up with her legs outstretched. But even if he was an arrogant brute of a man, he was, she reluctantly if gratefully conceded, a very gentle doctor, gloved fingers gently probing the swollen bruise, then pouring antiseptic fluid over the wound to clean it rather than probing it.

'You need a couple of stitches.'

'I don't!'

'When was your last tetanus injection?' he asked, completely ignoring her response.

'I can't remember.' Annie frowned. 'When I was training—eight, nine years ago, I guess.' She gave a rather pathetic shrug. She must give out fifty tetanus injections a day, and yet here she was not up to date.

'So you need a tetanus shot as well as stitches. I will put you on some antibiotics, too.'

'It's a small cut…'

'It's deep; it was sustained on the top of a damp shower cubicle. Tell me, when do you think the last time was that the cleaners went up on a ladder to disinfect the top of the partitions? Of course, we could leave it, wait and see.' He was scribbling on the pad as he wrote his orders. 'Maybe on Saturday you'll come back when it's swollen and infected and we can start you on them then. Oh, but you have a wedding to go to on Saturday, don't you?'

She didn't want stitches. Really, after the morning she'd had, all Annie wanted was to be left alone. But as he disappeared, returning moments later with a stainless-steel trolley laden with suture material and packs, all she could do was lie back and get it over with.

'Poor thing…' Cheryl tutted as she came in and headed to the sink to wash her hands before assisting. 'Let's hope it's OK for Saturday—we can't have you hobbling up the aisle behind Jackie.'

'There's no need for you to assist.' Iosef's tone was supremely polite but completely non-negotiable. 'I'm fine by myself.'

'Of course you are.' Cheryl gave a tight smile. 'But I'll just stay and keep Annie company for moral support.'

'I can manage that, too!' Iosef responded without looking up, draping Annie's leg and pulling on surgical gloves. 'Actually, could you bring me a sick certificate so I can sign her off for the rest of the day?'

Annie didn't even argue, rather grateful, in fact, for his display of brusqueness, because till now it had seemed solely reserved for her. But her mind was too fuddled to work that one out, though she was kind of relieved not to have a colleague holding her hand and murmuring the 'right' thing while Iosef stitched her up. Nobody needed to witness her grimacing over a few measly stitches when they witnessed so much worse every day. But, damn, it hurt.

'That's the worst over.' His voice was low and

soothing as he gave her a local injection. 'I'm gloved so I can't give you a tissue—there are some beside you.'

'I'm not crying.'

'Well, you can.'

She didn't say anything, didn't open her eyes and reach over, scared she would cry now he was being nice to her. Really nice to her. She heard him peel off his gloves, pull a couple of tissues from the box, which he pressed into her hand, before resanitising and opening up another pair of gloves.

'Sorry!' Annie sniffed, still refusing to cry but horribly, horribly close to it. 'It actually doesn't hurt that much.'

'Can you feel that?'

'What?'

'The needle I am sticking into your wound.' He caught her eyes as she started a touch, smiled at her for the very first time and waited till she managed a small watery smile back.

'It hasn't exactly been the best morning for you,' Iosef said.

'For you either,' Annie sniffed, 'but you're not close to tears.'

'Yes, but I'm an insensitive bastard— remember?'

He made her giggle—actually made her giggle—as he clipped the needle onto the suture holder. Maybe he was just being a doctor now, putting her at ease as he did all his patients. Which was as nice as it was confusing—making her like him when really she shouldn't.

'OK.' He turned his attention back to her leg. 'I'll get started.'

It shouldn't take long, all that was needed was a good clean-up and a couple of stitches, but he clearly planned to take his time, pulling a stool over with his foot and making himself comfortable before he started. And even though the silence was sort of comfortable, Annie still felt as if she ought to fill it with the sort of nervous chatter that always came when it wasn't needed.

'What was wrong with Mickey?'

'Who?'

'Mickey Baker, the patient you admitted to Obs on Monday.'

'The head injury?'

'That's the one—there was something else going on.'

'I can't remember.'

'Yes, you can.' She saw the edge of his mouth briefly twist in a smile.

'Check his notes.' Iosef shrugged. 'I really can't—'

'I tried to check his notes, only they're still signed out to you.'

'Oh.'

'So—where did you work?' Annie moved on, staring up at the rather dirty ceiling as she spoke, horrified at the view the patients had of the emergency Room. 'Before you came here.'

'Russia.'

'Oh.'

'Moscow.'

'For how long?'

'Five years.'

'Nice?'

There was an incredibly long pause, long enough for Annie to stop looking at the ceiling and drag her eyes to him.

'Not really.'

'But you stayed for five years.'

'And I should probably have stayed for a good few more.' He continued with the task in hand as he spoke, and though she couldn't see or feel anything she knew what he was doing, heard the snip of the scissors as he cut the thread of her stitches, saw him shift slightly and then the trickle of antiseptic on the bit of her leg that wasn't numb. 'There—you need these out in five days, perhaps a week. You can go to your own GP for that or have one of the nurses here—'

'Sure!' Annie sat up just a touch too quickly, tiny stars dancing in front of her eyes. And then there was the pressure of his hand pushing her back down.

'Rest here for a while. Have you had breakfast?'

'There wasn't exactly time!'

'You should make time,' he answered in a matter-of-fact voice. 'You need a drink and something to eat before you drive home.'

'I really could work. After this shift I'm off till Monday.'

'Good!' he said, snapping off his gloves. 'I'll see you on Monday. Or perhaps on Saturday if…' She felt her heart stop as he turned around, a massive blush spreading on her face as for a second, for a teensy-weensy momentary flight of fancy, she dared to dream he was about to ask her out. 'Jackie still wants me at the reception after this morning.'

'Finished?' Cheryl popped her head around the curtain and gave Annie a big smile. 'You've got a visitor, Iosef. She says it's personal.'

'Candy?' he asked, and Cheryl nodded.

'Thanks. See that Annie has a drink and something to eat before she drives home. Perhaps we can arrange a taxi.'

'I'm fine to drive,' Annie insisted. Still, she

did make her way to the canteen and, no matter the calories and a dress that didn't fit, rummaged for change in her pocket. She did the sensible thing and ordered a large mug of hot chocolate and a round of toast and enjoyed the peace for a few minutes, waiting for the queasy feeling in her stomach to subside before slowly heading out to her car.

Though where she thought she was going without her bag and car keys was anyone's guess.

Maybe she should get a taxi, Annie mused, limping back through the car park to the department to retrieve her bag from her locker.

Pale but a little more together, she slipped into the staffroom, deciding to leave through the obs ward than go through the rigmarole of saying goodbye. She almost instantly wished that she hadn't as she walked into the staffroom to find Iosef slouching against her locker, braving his second confrontation in less than an hour.

She was seriously beautiful.

It was the first thought that entered Annie's head as she swung in and saw Iosef up to his neck in long limbs and fabulous red hair, the ravishing woman crying in his arms so reed thin, so exquisitely dressed that Annie had never felt more drab or fat as, blushing, she stumbled out an apology for disturbing them. Not that Iosef said anything to her—and the ravishing Candy gave her barely more than an irritated glance as she turned her attention back to a more deserving cause.

'Please, don't do this, Iosef,' she sobbed. 'It's been so long. Tonight, please…'

'I'm working tonight and late every night this week.'

'The weekend, then.' Candy begged as Iosef pulled her aside slightly, just enough to allow Annie access to her locker.

'I have plans this weekend. Candy, I would really rather you stop coming here and disturbing my work.'

Bastard.

'So tell me when, then,' Candy sobbed as Annie's burning face dived into her locker.

'I'll try to ring you tomorrow.'

'Promise.'

'I just said that I would try—I'm not going to promise you anything.'

An honest bastard, though, Annie allowed. As Candy flounced off she realised they were alone—realised that had she shot out of the door just a couple of seconds earlier she wouldn't have had to face him till Monday when the embarrassment she was feeling now would be far less acute. She wouldn't be standing here now, shuffling her feet and wondering whether she should say anything—acknowledge what she'd just overheard or just mumble goodbye and thank him for the stitches!

'It's really not turning out to be your day, is it?' She settled for somewhere in between, and watched, quietly pleased as his crabby, angry face broke into a dry smile.

'Given the run that I am having—you'll

probably slap my face for saying it—but every woman I've come in contact with today is either premenstrual or I really need to lift my game.'

She didn't want him to make her laugh, didn't want him to be able to do that to her again, but he did.

Oh, he did.

'I think we'd have both have been better off if we'd just decided to spend the day in bed.' She knew what she had been trying to say and he knew what she had been trying to say, but somehow her perfectly innocent statement took on a double meaning as soon as it was delivered. She saw the light in his eyes, his eyes scorching hers as she rued every thoughtless word, as suddenly they were staring at each other and thinking only about one thing.

And she missed him being horrible to her.

Missed it because when he wasn't being nice or sexy or funny—as impossible as he was to deal with—that Iosef was a whole lot easier to deal with than this one.

'I'd better go…' She attempted a smile and a casual wave and tried to walk rather than run for the door, biting on her bottom lip as for just a fraction of a second he stalled her at the door with his answer.

'You'd better!'

The combination of the diet, the pain and the anaesthetic must have fuddled her brain, Annie decided later as she arrived at the church where Jackie was barking orders like a sergeant major. As if someone as divine, gorgeous and utterly dismissive as Dr Gorgeous had really been flirting that morning. It had been a miscommunication—just a funny little thing that if it had been anyone else, had it been, say George, they'd both just have laughed.

As if Iosef Kolovsky, who had the pick of the worlds truly beautiful people would even be remotely interested in a rather plain, rather neurotic nurse.

As if someone as well heeled, well groomed

and utterly fabulous as Iosef wouldn't have a ravishing beauty on his arm.

That was what the Kolovskys were famous for after all—it was in their blood.

His elder brother Levander had had more women than the tabloids could keep up with till his recent marriage, and it was an open secret that Ivan had had a string of extramarital affairs. Why wouldn't Iosef have the requisite super-model on ice, frantically waiting for the master to call…?

And why did it matter so much to *her*?

'Over here, Annie.' Jackie was jangling with nerves as she shifted her two millimetres to the right. 'I want you in front of Claudia and Bella the flower girl… Oh, where the hell's Iosef?'

'Iosef?' Annie couldn't help but ask.

'I left my wedding folder in my office—Iosef said he'd drop it round once Marshall arrived. And Jeremy's best man is stuck doing an emergency appendectomy. The whole rehearsal is turning into a disaster. We really can't start till he gets here, so I'll just run through a couple of details, if that's OK.'

Annie really wished she wouldn't or at the very least that they could sit down for it. She already knew that they were to exfoliate tonight for their spray tan at ten tomorrow, that they weren't to wash their hair again after tonight so that it stayed up beautifully on Saturday. Her leg was starting to throb again and apart from that glass of hot chocolate and toast and thanks to a rather extended midday nap, she hadn't had another calorie all day.

'Your dress fits OK?' Jackie's headlamps were thankfully on Claudia.

'It's fabulous.' The *tiny* Claudia beamed.

'Annie?'

'It looks marvellous!' Annie assured her, crossing her fingers and praying that it would. But Jackie wasn't listening, that morning's exchange clearly forgiven and forgotten as she greeted her saviour.

'Iosef! Thank goodness!'

Goodness indeed!

So far Annie had seen him in a suit and she winced, caught a stolen glimpse of him in bathers. But a spot of blood or something must have found its way onto his usually immaculate attire, because he was dressed in theatre blues and a pair of runners and he looked... divine!

Apart from that little peek from a distance at the pool she'd only been privy to him from his Adam's apple upwards, but now his arms were on show, pale, toned arms that had a just enough dark hair to make her toes curl. Thanks to the lack of budget in the laundry department, threadbare pants outlined rather muscular thighs and a pert bottom that she really shouldn't be noticing.

'Could I ask a huge favour, Iosef?' Jackie didn't wait for an answer before she plunged in. 'Brian's stuck in Theatre till heaven knows when—would you mind filling in as best man?'

Annie couldn't help smiling sympathetically as he gamely agreed.

Wedding rehearsals are possibly the most futile of futile exercises, Annie concluded more than an hour later—all they did was leave everyone feeling worse!

Everything that could go wrong did—and it was impossible to imagine that in just two days this motley crew could somehow shape up to become a suitable wedding party. The flower girl's bedtime had long since passed and she was in floods of tears, the vicar was glancing at his watch and wondering if he'd ever get dinner, yet Jackie was grim with determination, insisting they run through it just one more time as the bullet of an antibiotic Annie had taken before she'd left continued to sit in her empty stomach and was starting to make her feel sick.

'And, *please*, Annie, could you remember to smile?'

Before or after I throttle you? Annie thought, poking her tongue out as Jackie turned her back and then feeling childish and stupid for doing so. For the briefest of seconds she caught Iosef's

eye. He was standing at the altar, looking thoroughly bored, but when he rolled his eyes Annie
actually managed a tiny giggle. She walked
behind the exhausted flower girl as Jackie
hummed the Wedding March ahead of them,
Jeremy beaming at his soon-to-be bride as she
arrived at the altar and Iosef rather inappropri-
ately yawning. Annie never really knew how it
happened, but those tiny little dots that had
danced in front of her eyes this morning
suddenly appeared again—only this time there
was no Iosef to push her back down onto a pillow
and no amount of blinking seemed to clear them.
Her lips were impossibly dry, but she could feel
herself sweating, feel herself gulping air in as she
willed herself not to faint.

'That's enough!' From somewhere she could
hear Iosef's voice as she let her eyes close—not
the best idea as the spinning in her head got faster
and Annie realised she was going to hit the floor.

'I really have to go, Jackie…'

Suddenly an arm was around her waist, Iosef

lifting her a good two inches off the floor and half carrying her, half briskly walking her the long length of the aisle before sitting her on a bench outside the church and rather unceremoniously shoving her head between her knees.

'Deep breaths—come on.'

'I'm going to be sick.'

'You're not. Just breathe slowly in and out through your mouth...' His hand was still pushing her head down. It was all very well for him to say she wasn't going to be sick, Annie thought in panic, but the deep breaths actually did start to work and she realised in relief she wasn't going to be *totally* humiliated.

'Big breaths.'

'Oh, God...' She was starting to think now as blood seeped back to her brain, and her nausea receded, embarrassment crept in. 'Did everyone see?'

'No one noticed, things were finishing up anyway. When did you last eat?'

'I don't know.' Her brain was still fuzzy, her

lips still dry and his hand was still pushing her head down.

'You haven't eaten anything, have you?' Iosef demanded. 'Silly girl…' Despite the fog, his words irritated her and she attempted to lift her head, but still he held it down. 'I've seen you— eating nothing all day or nibbling on a small salad when there is cheesecake someone's bought in…'

'I don't like cheesecake.'

'Oh, but you love your lettuce, don't you? What are you doing at the gym twice a day? Just what the hell is it with you women, just what are you trying to achieve?'

'I really don't need a lecture.' His hand was off her head and gingerly Annie sat up and tried to explain, but Iosef wasn't even going to pretend to listen.

'Oh, but I think you do. I think you need someone to give you a proper talking to. How do you expect to do a full-time job and—?'

'Annie…' Claudia came over, her face working up as if she was about to cry.

'I'm fine.' Annie smiled, but Annie's near faint wasn't what was on Claudia's mind.

'Look, please, don't breathe a word to Jackie. If I'm wrong, it's fine—I'll sort something out— but when you said your dress fitted marvellously…' The two women's eyes met in shock, both literally drooping in relief as realisation hit.

'Your dress doesn't fit either?' A grin started to spread across her pale face.

'It's just way too big. I'm sorry, I didn't mean it like that. When I say it's *way* too big…'

'Don't apologise.' Annie almost wept in relief. 'I've been dieting like crazy all week, hitting the gym morning and night…'

'Tell me about it—I've been eating takeaways three times a day and spending a fortune on padded bras…' Claudia groaned.

'You two have mixed up your dresses?' And though she wasn't actually talking to him—was still smarting from his words—Iosef persisted in spite of her rather pointedly looking away. 'That is why you have been on this crazy diet?'

'Why else?' Annie snapped, then turned her attention back to Claudia. 'Do you want to bring it over and swap now?'

'Is tomorrow OK?' Claudia shook her head. 'I'm supposed to be going to Mum's after here.'

'Sure.' Annie gave a pale smile, still a touch woolly but feeling a whole lot better. 'I'll see you at the hairdresser's in the morning.'

'Let's get you home.' For the second time that day Iosef questioned her ability to drive, only this time it was non-negotiable. 'I'll drop you off.'

'I'm OK…'

'You are certainly not OK—you've nearly fainted twice today. And I really don't fancy being called into work because you've caused a major pile-up, making your own way home. Come on!'

Should she ask him in?

For the whole of the short drive home Annie worried over the question. If it had been *any* other colleague, then, of course, she'd offer. But somehow the thought of him seeing her rather shabby flat was, well…embarrassing.

Not that it was left up to her.

Instead of dropping her off, instead of an awkward silence while he waited for her to be polite, Iosef pulled into the driveway and, switching off the engine, climbed straight out, walking with her to the doorstep. When she fumbled with her keys he took them from her, opened the door, and without invitation or consideration took her by the elbow and led her in.

'Where's your kitchen?' He frowned at her bemused expression. 'Given I can't trust you to follow my orders without supervision, I guess I'm going to have to fix you something to eat myself. Now, go and sit down and I will bring you some supper.'

'Hold on a minute…' Annie started, but it was already too late. He brushed past her and stalked through to her kitchen, and it was either follow him and engage in a pointless argument or take the few moments' grace to attempt a quick clean-up of the living room.

'Do you get some sort of kick out of ignoring my advice?'

'No…' Flustered, she turned around a mountain of magazines and had a whole load of ironing in her hand as he stood menacingly in the doorway. She had no idea how long he'd been watching—if he'd seen her kick her bras under the sofa and polish the table with her sleeve…' I was just…' Her voice trailed off and, placing her load on the coffee-table, she finally followed his orders, sitting down on the sofa and actually stretching out her legs, blinking in surprise when, from the hell of her kitchen, he emerged with buttered toast and some mushroom soup she'd long forgotten was even there!

'Eat it all!'

And two mouthfuls in, Annie realised just how hungry she really was, doing as she was told and even mopping the plate with her toast.

'How long have you been on this diet?'

'Since Monday.' Annie gave an embarrassed shrug. 'You've seen what Jackie's like. Could you imagine having to tell her that the dress didn't fit? So Melanie and I came up with a plan…' He didn't answer her nervous chatter, just stared at her through narrowed eyes, watching her closely as she spoke. 'Anyway, it turns out that it was just a mix-up. It's all fine now.'

'But you didn't eat anything at all today.'

'I had some toast at work… I just forgot, OK?' Annie snapped. 'What with my leg and the rehearsal and everything…'

'You *forgot* to eat.'

'Yes.' She gave a tiny little cough as she said it, didn't like the way he was staring at her, as if somehow he knew better…as if somehow he knew her secret!

'You didn't *forget* to go to the gym, though!' Annie didn't answer, just sat in a long embarrassing silence, an unbecoming blush creeping across her face as he continued to glare at her.

'It's no big deal…' Her voice was a croak and again she had to cough to clear it. 'It was just for a week.'

'Good!' Lecture over, he stood up and so too did Annie, against orders.

'I can see myself out.'

'Good!' Annie replied. 'And I can see myself to bed.'

They walked rather uncomfortably along her narrow hall, Annie in front, achingly aware of him behind her, his unbelievable presence in her tiny flat completely overwhelming.

'Do you need a lift in the morning?' he queried. 'It's no problem for me to drop you off at your car on my way to work.'

'I'll be fine.' Annie smiled. 'I'll ring Claudia and have her pick me up.'

'Go to bed, then.'

'I will.' Her face was nearly cracking from smiling, from pretending she was OK—he couldn't possibly have known how much his earlier words had stung, the wretched shame she was feeling at this very moment... Or maybe he did know.

'Don't play dangerous games with your health, Annie.'

'I wasn't.' Her heart was hammering in her chest, tears suddenly horribly close again—embarrassed tears, though, like being caught with your hand in the cookie jar—or, to be more accurate in her case, refusing to put your hand into the cookie jar, as if he'd somehow become privy to her dark secrets. A shaking hand raked through her hair, and she was tempted to push him out the door and slam it shut. How did he know what a dangerous game she'd been playing this week? How could he possibly have known that murky piece of her past when every calorie had been counted and exercised away, where every piece of her flesh had been critically scrutinised and loathed. 'It really was just for one week…' Annie closed her eyes for a second. 'And today was just an oversight…' Her voice faded, because she had been quite a silly girl this week.

Or, rather, a silly woman.

She should have known that with her past a

crash diet was something she should never have toyed with.

She wanted him to go, wanted him the hell away from her, the tears she'd held back all day spilling out now, and she didn't want him to see.

But he did.

The man who had kept her at arm's length all week suddenly pulled her in, and when he wrapped her in his embrace, it was such a sweet relief to give in.

And suddenly the last thing she wanted was for him to go—her heart was hammering again, her breath coming hard and fast, but for entirely different reasons now. She'd never been held like this. Even if she knew she should push away, she didn't want to. For the first time in the longest time, for the first time in for ever perhaps, she didn't have to pretend, at least for a minute or two.

'Go to bed.' His words were soft, it was the nicest he'd ever spoken to her. The pad of his thumb wiped away a few stray tears. But he was just being nice, wiping away her tears like he would those of a niece or a cousin, because a man like Iosef Kolovsky could never look at someone like her as a woman. So why then were his lips on hers, why wasn't she gasping in shock at his audacity, why, why why, were her own lips moving to his? The velvet of his flesh was on hers and it was as soothing as it was disturbing—because if ever there was a perfect kiss she'd found it now. There was none of the awkwardness that usually accompanied a first kiss— no ducking to the left as he moved to the right, almost like kissing a long-time lover, his touch, his mouth *familiar* almost. But never, not for a single second as his tongue chased hers, not for a single second as his hand pressed her face deeper to his, was it *accustomed*, each stroke of his tongue, each taste of him causing a mini-riot inside her. The only awkwardness was in a mind that was whirling frantically, yet her mouth, her body was utterly at peace with the barrage of sensations he delivered. And most unfamiliar of all—for someone so gauche, for someone light years in experience from the man she was kissing—was the inner confidence, this deep primeval knowing almost, as she kissed him back, that he was lost in it too. Enjoying, relishing it just as much as she was, and as she pulled away and stared long, long into those gorgeous eyes, she knew that no other kiss would ever equal the sheer perfection of this one.

'Go to bed.'

She could taste him on her lips, her tongue running over them, sucking in the last dregs, seeing her own moisture around his full mouth and shamelessly wanting to kiss it off. Impetuous decisions took but a second to come to, and her mouth opened to deliver a reckless offer.

'Bed!' He barked the order, cutting off whatever she was about to say, and turned and slammed the door shut. She wasn't upset or disappointed at his rapid departure, just stunned at the turn of events. She stood in her hallway, her heart leaping inside, veins thrumming, twitching with lust, stunned, incredulous as she savoured again every delicious, breathless, silent moment.

That was his kiss!

If that was his kiss, what the hell would it be like to make love with him?

CHAPTER FIVE

IT *WAS* a fabulous wedding!

All the meticulous preparations paid off in the end. The bride was glowing, the flower girl was adorable and the bridesmaids were stunning!

Despite Annie's reservations, the spray-on tan hadn't turned her orange and her hair was still perfectly in place when the speeches ended and the dancing started.

'Thank God that's over…' Melanie was working her way down a bottle of champagne and frantically looking around to see where George was. 'Do you think we'll get the old Jackie back now?'

'Don't be mean.' Annie laughed. 'We're all grateful for her relentless attention to detail when it comes to the patients—that's just the way she is.'

'Do you think George likes me?' Melanie asked, looking longingly over to where he stood in a little group.

'You know he likes you.'

'Well, do you think he's ever going to do something about it?'

'Why wait for him?' Annie asked. 'Go and ask him to dance.'

'No way!' Melanie said indignantly. 'If he wants to dance, he can ask me!'

'And I thought you were such a modern woman!' Annie pointed out.

'Well, some traditions are fine just as they are.' Even as Melanie answered, her attention was distracted from George. Her eyes, like those of every other female in the room, were turning to the door where Iosef was making a rather late but spectacular entrance. Annie could feel her heart relocate to her mouth as he walked towards Jackie and gave her a kiss then shook Jeremy's hand. She found herself waiting, bracing herself almost for the fabulous Candy to suddenly appear beside him, but by the time he'd shaken a few hands and kissed a few cheeks, it was clear that he'd come alone.

'He's just gorgeous!' Melanie sighed.

'I thought you liked George.'

'George is a keeper…' Melanie explained her strange logic. 'Iosef would be a forgivable crime of passion. Don't tell me you haven't thought about him, too.'

'Not really.' Annie blushed beneath her foundation—he was all she'd thought about since that blistering kiss! 'I mean, yes, he's good-looking and all that, but he can be really rude at times.'

'Which is why he isn't a keeper!' Melanie explained patiently. 'Oh, my goodness, he's coming this way.' Jumping up in delight as he approached and braver than she'd been about asking George to dance, she simply stepped into Iosef's arms and Annie was left a sudden wallflower as Iosef danced with her friend.

With *all* her friends.

He was actually a great dancer, Annie observed

as he worked his way through the women, and she didn't know if he was teasing her or tempting her, but whatever it was it was cruel. No matter how hard she tried to ignore him, no matter how hard she pretended not to care, or how busy and full her evening was, she was at every turn supremely conscious of him.

Supremely conscious that he wasn't even looking at her!

He'd kissed her because he could, Annie decided long after Jackie had left, when the crowd was starting to thin and she was dancing with George, but her mind was a million miles away. Iosef had kissed her because, no doubt, that's what he did best—he'd probably forgotten all about it by the time he'd hit home. Not for a second would it have had the same sort of impact on him.

'Should I ask her out?' George was dancing with Annie but gazing over at Melanie. And Annie was dancing with George and trying not to look over to where Iosef was dancing with Beth.

'Of course you should.' Annie nodded, giving up on being subtle because the two of them were driving her crazy.

'I'll ask her at work on Monday,' George said firmly, as Annie just rolled her eyes.

'No, you won't. Why don't you go over there and ask her now?'

'Now?' George blinked as the music ended.

'Now!'

'Oh, hello, sir, I mean Iosef…' George gratefully jumped at the diversion of Iosef walking past. 'Great wedding, isn't it?'

'It's been OK. I'm just going to head off home now…' And from somewhere George must have found his courage because without a single word he bolted off towards Melanie, leaving Annie standing with Iosef on the dance floor, feeling horribly awkward as the music started up again.

'Dance?'

'I've had enough of duty for one day!'

'Stop sulking.' Iosef grinned.

'I'm not.'

'Stop sulking and dance.'

It unsettled her how relieved she felt.

How blissful it felt to be in his arms, and the effects of a week of little food was nothing to the dizzying heights he took her to.

'I've actually been wanting to dance with you all night.' His low whisper made her ears tickle and she squirmed in pleasure but tried to stay cool.

'Then why didn't you?'

'Same as you—duty first.'

And because he'd danced with everyone, because he'd worked the room, no one gave them a second glance, and for that Annie was grateful, grateful too to just close her eyes and sway to the music with him. She could feel the heat of his palm in the small of her back, feel his warm breath on her bare shoulder, his heavy scent filling her nostrils. Combined with the intoxicating memory of his lips on hers, the combination was lethal.

'You look amazing!'

'Thanks.' He wasn't the first to have told her that, Annie reminded herself—after all it was

obligatory for people to say that to the bridesmaids. 'I don't always look this good.'

'Modest, too!' He laughed.

'I didn't mean that...' She shook her head
against his shoulder. How could she explain that
this rather passable parcel was down to weeks of
preparation, that the very groomed woman he
held in his arms was an absolute one-off?

He lowered his head slightly, so close his chin
was dusting her cheek as he whispered in the
shell of her ear.

'You smell amazing.'

Now, *that* wasn't expected—she could feel her
throat tighten, a knot of anticipation tightening
in her stomach as his breath tickled her ear.

'You feel amazing.' There was just a small
increase of pressure on her back. Her stomach
curled inside. She almost wept in frustration as
the slow music stopped and couples stood back
a fraction and clapped or frantically ran for
freedom. Annie knew she ought to go. This man
was so potently sexual it would be so, so easy to

say or do something she might regret, so pathetically easy to misread the signs and make an utter fool of herself.

And anyway he had a girlfriend.

Thanking him, she turned to go, desperate almost for the normality of Melanie or the safety of the loos, where she could splash her burning face in cool water, but Iosef caught her hand.

'Where are you going?'

'I ought to—'

'You ought to relax.' He gave a lazy smile. 'Jackie's gone, your duties are all over, you can enjoy the last dance. Anyway…' he pulled her back to him '…it would be *very* rude to leave me like this!'

She didn't know what he meant, not sure if she'd misunderstood, but as his hands drew her in, as her body returned from whence it had been, like a dint in the pillow, her head returned to its rightful place, she knew that she hadn't misinterpreted, knew for sure that she hadn't when he held her just that little bit closer.

'Let's hope this is a very long dance…' His voice was low and husky in her ear—shockingly inappropriate but so very, very sexy. He brushed against her as they moved. She could see her colleagues drifting past as they danced or sat on the sidelines and chatted. Perhaps there'd be a few nudges, but he'd danced with enough women to ensure the spotlight wasn't on them now and not a single person watching would have guessed what was going on before their eyes.

She'd never felt like this.

Just dancing with him mocked a hundred times over the efforts of lovers who had quickly come and gone! Arousal coursed through her, thick arousal that moved slowly through her body, stirring her as it went, each throb of the music resonating through her body, each breath, each movement of her chest somehow unfathomably provocative, *his* breath shorter now in her ear.

'I want to kiss you.'

'You can't.'

'But I want to.'

'Well…' She could hardly breathe, let alone speak. 'You can't.'

'Not your lips.' Iosef's mouth painted a decadent picture as still he whispered in her ear. 'Your skin.'

'You can't.' She could hardly get the words out, knowing she'd regret it—not the kiss but the audience.

'Since that night all I want is to kiss you again…'

Which put paid to the theory he'd forgotten. Oh, and she wanted him to kiss her, wanted his mouth on her shoulder, wanted to press herself against him so badly it was indecent, she could hardly swallow, the air so thick with lust, her breasts stinging as they strained at her dress, and as the music stilled, as the lights came on, Annie felt like she was waking up from some erotic dream, the hotel ballroom full of limp balloons and plates of half-eaten food, a thousand dirty glasses littering the tables and in front of her, a rather red-faced Melanie holding George's hand.

'I know we were going to share a taxi but

George has offered to give me a lift.' Her eyes were wide with apology and pleading. 'Though we can drop you off first.'

'It's a bit out of your way…' Annie smiled. 'I'll get my own taxi.'

'I guess I can give you a lift home—do you live near?'

Iosef said it so reluctantly that if they hadn't just been on the dance floor, Annie would have sworn he was just being reluctantly polite, not that Melanie cared. 'You're an angel, Iosef. ''Night, then…' She practically ran out of the ballroom, but by the time Annie had collected her bag, it didn't seem such a good idea any more. OK, he'd seen her tiny flat, but she couldn't possibly ask him back now, could she? And what if…?

'I'm just going to the ladies'.'

'Sure.'

It was one of those completely fabulous ladies' rooms—discreet music filling the perfumed air, mirrors everywhere, baskets full of fluffy white hand towels even at this late hour. Despite not needing to use the loo, Annie used her time wisely. She drew a deep breath as she stared in the mirror at her flushed face—and unlike Melanie it had nothing to do with too much champagne.

Her thick, glossy, for once straight hair fell over one heavily made-up eye, her body was a delicious golden brown, even her lipstick was still on—never again would she look this good and never again would she have the opportunity to spend the night with someone as divine as Iosef Kolovsky.

It would never work… Running her wrists under the tap, Annie gave herself a harsh talking to.

She'd surely regret it in the morning.

She worked with him, for heaven's sake. Imagine facing him on Monday…

No, she'd tell him thanks very much for the offer, but she'd take a taxi home.

Pulling the door open, she stepped out into the foyer with resolve, jumping slightly when from the shadows he caught her wrist.

'I was thinking—'

'Don't.' His lips were moving in on her and there was nowhere to go except against the wall.

'Maybe we should…' She didn't finish the sentence. His mouth was where her neck met her shoulder, and like a reflex action Annie's head arched to the side, her eyes closing as his tongue worked its magic. 'Maybe…I…should…' Each word was an effort, each word forced out between breaths, each word refuted by the body that was wilting before him. 'Just…get…a…taxi…'

'Why?' He came up for air, pinning her with his eyes,

'Because…we might regret it…'

'We might…' He kissed her, his tongue forcing her lips apart, stroking her as if he were stroking her somewhere deep inside, then coming up for air, slowly licking his lips as if tasting her again. 'But I'll definitely regret it if we don't. I've wanted you since I saw you.'

'You weren't nice…'

'Doesn't mean I didn't want you.'

Don't play dangerous games. He'd told her that himself, warned her perhaps of what she was taking on, and he *was* dangerous.

Brooding, autocratic and lethally sexy, she knew nothing about him, yet she craved more.

'You've been…' She could hardly breathe, hardly get the words out. 'Ignoring me.'

'You try to resist what is bad for you—*that* is what I've been doing.'

'How could I be bad for you?' She gave a tiny shrill giggle, but Iosef wasn't laughing. He pressed her harder against the wall, his lips working up along her neck, making her shiver as he spoke between hot kisses.

'It is foolish to get involved with someone you work with.'

'I know!' Annie breathed.

'I am not available for a relationship.'

'You're seeing someone?'

'I'm not available for anyone…'

'Candy?' Bravely she voiced the question, the single word halting him in mid-kiss. Passion flushed features coming into focus as he raised his head to hers.

'There is nothing there for you to concern yourself with.'

'But I do…' She should have persisted, Annie knew that, should have asked for clarification, should have made damn sure she knew exactly how deep the water was before she dived in, but his lips were on her shoulders again, his parted mouth kissing her flesh so deeply it hurt, actually, deliciously, hurt. Lust was the deadliest of sins, Annie decided when finally he pulled back, his pupils dilated, his full mouth moist from their kiss. Reaching in his pocket, he held up a key.

Lust was surely the deadliest sin because it so readily paved the way for others—and greed was the first to make itself known. She wanted him so much, so fiercely, that her self-control was completely shot. He lowered his head, kissed the top of her cleavage, kissed it so deeply she thought she might come right there, right there in the shadows of the lobby, her breath catching as his fingers pushed the cool metal key between them, her nipples so hard she nearly wept for the cool of his mouth.

'I've booked you a room.'

'Me?' Annie gulped, and he nodded.

'This time,' he said slowly, 'I want you to ask me in.'

CHAPTER SIX

AN OLD-FASHIONED lift hurtled them to the top floor as Annie's blood pressure did the same. The doors finally opened and they stepped into a hallway with gorgeous mosaic tiles that echoed as she walked along and came to the room he'd booked for her.

'Do you need a hand?'

Her hands were shaking so much she probably did. Any fantasy she had of suavely opening the door and inviting him in vanished in a puff of smoke when he witnessed her rather clumsy efforts at retrieval. But he was in absolutely no rush to go anywhere, making her task near impossible as he shamelessly pulled down the zipper of her dress, his fingers taking down the straps. Shocked, aroused, her eyes searched the deserted corridor for a night porter, her breath heaving in hard, quick gasps as she soon stood naked from the waist up except for a flimsy bra.

'Someone might come,' Annie gasped.

'Then you'd better hurry up and get inside.'

Her lacy bra was the target of his attentions now. His head lowered and his mouth closed in on one nipple through the flimsy material, then pulled back just enough to voice his question. 'Well—are you going to ask me in?'

Annie took a breath, trying, and failing, to gather her chaotic thoughts.

His fingers were inside her bra now, one spray-tanned breast standing erect and quivering with freedom. At last, she retrieved the key and, holding it up, caught the glint of triumph in his eyes as she stood before him drenched in desire and trepidation. Since she'd first laid eyes on him, Annie had wanted him. He was out of her league, she would never have knowingly pursued him, but she must have been flirting, sending out tiny subliminal messages that clearly he'd registered. Like teasing a panther in the zoo, waving and poking out her tongue with the assurance of a locked door—but now he was out of the cage, now this sleek beautiful, untamed animal was pressing her to the wall and ready to play…

Trembling fingers somehow pushed the key into the lock and turned it, registering that she was terrified of the beast she'd unleashed but excited nonetheless.

'I'm not…' She attempted to be straight with him, her wide eyes taking in the vast bed, her body a quivering bundle of nerves and desire, positive, positive she wasn't up to the challenge but frantic to attempt it. 'Iosef, I'm not…'

'Not what?'

He was kissing her again, pushing her already unzipped dress up over her bottom till she stood only in Jackie's outrageous choice of underwear and a great wad of mocha silk around her waist. His hands ran over her suspenders and dug into her bottom and she closed her eyes in horror at the thought of the firm, toned bottoms he was surely more used to encountering. The nubile, sophisticated, experienced lovers he was surely used to, the women who would know how to excite him. Woefully sure she didn't fit the bill, that for him disappointment could only ensue, panic fizzed inside her. 'I'm not very good at making love!' There, she'd said it. Her admission had been delivered in a shrill voice, her apology for teasing him, for playing with fire all there in that rapid, short sentence. Only he didn't seem to be listening. Instead, he was kissing her with more force. His hands had left her bottom and were by his sides, only their lips in contact, but with so much force that if she didn't want to topple over then she had no choice but to move backwards. Any further attempt to speak was silenced by his mouth, then the back of the bed was pressing into her thighs. She had nowhere to go except the bed, but he didn't let her fall, instead cupping her bottom again as he pressed her heat to his, his fierce erection a taste of what was to come as he brushed away her excuses.

'*I* do the making!'

And, boy, did he!

Sixteen and a half years ago her sister had done her homework for her.

And sixteen years ago she'd had to sit through speech day—had had to accept an award for work she hadn't done, had wanted to stand up in front of a terrifying crowd and admit she really didn't deserve it, hadn't done a single thing to merit it, actually.

The random memory popped into her mind as this gorgeous man pushed her down on the bed. She was tempted to stand up and declare that she really wasn't *that* good, that she really didn't merit such attention as his mouth worked his way up her thighs, kissing and nibbling her soft flesh through silk stockings, that she really wasn't that deserving…

'You taste fantastic…' Even though she had her panties on it didn't stop him. He pulled them to one side, his tongue doing wicked things, dotting the i in the most decadent of ways, pushing, tearing fifteen hundred dollars' worth of mocha silk over her head and dispensing with her bra. He was so into her, so consuming, so blatant with his adoration, so feverishly good it was impossible not to feel amazing.

It was impossible not to feel the most wanton sexual being, when the most wanton, sexual being of them all thought that you were. 'Oh, Annie…' Over and over he said it as he tasted her, over and over he said it as his mouth worked its way upwards, kissing her stomach, her breasts, her neck, her lips as she writhed beneath him. 'I have wanted you so much…'

Wow!

It was her last coherent thought as he sucked on her shoulder, her last grasp at reality as he plunged inside her, and for Annie it should have been over, tightening muscles dragging him in, her mind whirring as she screamed his name. But Iosef was as good as his word, Iosef still doing the making, kissing her, teasing her, as he bucked deep inside her, taking her to the heights then starting the ride all over again.

CHAPTER SEVEN

'LEVANDER'S the one who just got married?'

They were lying in the rumpled bed—dawn still a little way off—warm and relaxed and thoroughly exhausted. Never had Annie felt more wonderful, lying unabashed and utterly adored in his arms, giggling as they spoke in intimate whispers.

'He lives in the UK now—Aleksi is back here in Australia.'

'Your twin?' Annie checked. 'Does he look like you?'

'Of course.' Iosef smiled. 'I told you—we're identical. Though our personalities are different.'

'In what way?'

'He can be a bit arrogant, moody…' His lips curved into a smile as she raised her eyebrows.

'I am nothing like that!' Iosef said indignantly. 'Aleksi is very driven, focused…' Giving in as her brows rose higher, he gave a low laugh. 'Maybe we are similar after all.'

'Gee!' Anne blew her fringe skywards as she considered the impossible. 'Do you think I'd be able to tell the….' Her voice trailed off as she decided that her question was rather unsuitable, but Iosef just laughed.

He was toying with her nipple. Tender and raw from earlier attention, he was drawing it out to an indecent length,

'To you he would look different…' Staring up at her from between her breasts, he registered her frown. 'If you had a twin, it would be the same for me.'

'How?' It should have been an easy question, but it gasped out of her lips as his fingers crept to the warmth between her legs, incessant fingers back on her swollen flesh which was sore and tender from his attention.

'Have I hurt you?'

'No.'

Yes.

Her mind wrestled for an answer. The tenderness was a small price to pay for the sensations she had experienced, so she diverted him with a question of her own. 'How would you know it wasn't me?'

'Because I've tasted you, smelt you, felt you in ways only you and I know…' He was rolling onto his back now, leaving her needy, twitching with the desire he so easily evoked. The sheet slipped down to reveal his morning glory and if she was tender, still she was wanting him, any soreness fading in the wake of her growing desire.

She ran her fingers along his length and he shuddered at her touch, the palm of her hand catching his full arousal, stroking his velvet skin, her throat catching as he gasped.

'*Patsihonku.*'

'Pardon?'

'I said to go more slowly.'

'Why?'

It was perhaps the most provocative of questions, but that was how he made her feel—daring, sexy. But as she slipped over him, her thighs astride his, suddenly she wasn't so sure. Naked, exposed over him, it was easy to chide herself…easy to reproach the woman he had made her. But as his hands held her hips, as he steadied her as he nudged at her entrance, it was harder to resist the way he made her feel.

Amazing, wanted, desired.

And now…

She could feel him swell inside her.

The mahogany of his nipple grabbed her attention, a tiny taste, a little bite as his hips moved beneath her,

She'd never been so bold but, then, she'd never been with anyone so beautiful.

And he really was.

Her eyes down, she was so ready to play—could see him sliding into her…

She *wanted* to tease him.

Wanted to lean forward, to jiggle her nipples over his mouth, *knew* what to do.

'Annie…' His mouth was grabbing at her breasts, his hips thrusting into her. 'We need…'

Her hands, his hands were both fumbling for the drawer, a futile task when he was so deep inside her. She didn't want him to stop, didn't want him to pull out, but he was. His hands pulled her bottom up—his delicious length reluctantly slipping out and pressing against damp curls. And then it was too late. The beats of her orgasm matched his as he spilled outside her, the heat of his semen, the sight of him overflowing as he pulsed beneath her, the groan of her name as he shot towards her.

'Annie—why now?'

Dark eyes begged a question that in the throes of orgasm Annie didn't even think to answer—Ioscf's fingers massaging his silken gift into her pliant flesh. 'Why do you have to do this to me now?'

CHAPTER EIGHT

SUNLIGHT was cruel.

In their haste they hadn't even thought about the curtains and as the morning sun crept across the rumpled room, instead of brightening things, everything seemed to dim. The craziness of last night was not so straightforward in the cold light of day.

'I have an appointment...' Leaning over, he picked up his watch from the bedside table. 'And I am on call tonight.'

'Sure.' She tried a wobbly smile, her hand inching across the bed to touch him, then moving back before it reached its destination, knowing somehow that the distance was suddenly too great. Instead she lay there, staring at the ceiling as he headed for the shower, listening to him curse as he shaved and wondering what the hell had suddenly gone wrong.

'I think you're the one who needs stitches today.' She attempted a joke as he came out of the shower, a white towel around his hips and a red blob of tissue on his cheek.

'Bloody hotel razors!'

Then there was the horrible indignity of having to put back on her bridesmaid's dress and shoes and bundle the rest of her things into a hotel laundry bag—but at least he waited till the car had been brought round before she had to suffer the shame of walking through a hotel reception area at eight a.m. on a Sunday morning dressed in last night's clothes. She felt sick and tried to read his closed mind as she pulled on her seat belt and sat in silence as he pulled his car out onto the road.

There was a line.

And he'd crossed it.

Comparing what had taken place with Annie

with a very brief review of all the women he'd been with, Iosef knew *beyond doubt* that he'd crossed it last night.

They hadn't just had sex.

Sex was about need— Sex was about want.

Yes, they'd had sex last night—but they'd had lot more besides.

As the traffic light turned green and he indicated to turn onto the freeway, Iosef attempted reason.

Guovano.

The expletive was there on his lips but he swallowed it down.

Why on earth had he gone to the wedding? And if he had had to go, he should have danced with her first, been polite, got it over with.

He glanced over at her.

Saw that pinched face trying to be brave.

Saw the unmistakable angry flush on her cheek as she pointedly stared out of the window.

And he was hard again.

Wanted to kiss away the doubts that were surely on her mind,

Wanted to make love to her, tell her she was crazy to even think such things.

More than that, he wanted to talk to her, to tell her all that was going on in his life.

Wanted the permission to talk without the pillow.

She'd never get it.

'I told you I could not have a relationship.'

'You did.' She was fiddling with radio stations—changing from the talkback show he listened to to some blasted pop, but he could still see the glint of tears in her eyes.

'It's just not possible at the moment.'

'You don't have to explain yourself to me.'

His knuckles were white as they gripped the steering-wheel, tempted to indicate, to pull over into the hard lane of the freeway and do just that: explain how impossible things were at the moment. Tell her why he couldn't be with her— only he couldn't.

'I'm no good for you.'

'On the contrary, I think you're very good for me.'

Hell, why couldn't she just get it? Why wasn't she spiteful now, demanding even, why couldn't she be like everyone else?

She expected to be let down.

He could see it as they pulled into the kerb, could see the jut of her jaw as she attempted casual.

'See you at work.'

'No doubt.' He gave her a wry smile, watched as her shaking hands pushed a few times on the window buttons before locating the door lock.

'Annie.' He caught her wrist as she was about to get out. 'I'd only make you miserable.'

'You just have, anyway.'

He should just let her walk away.

Let her trip up her straight garden path wearing a bridesmaid's dress and a few love bites, not entertain thoughts of letting her in on his twisted life; treat her coolly today so that by Monday she had got the message—only he couldn't.

Couldn't actually bring himself to do it to *her*.

'Annie…' As she turned around and hopeful

eyes shot to his, he wanted to tell her that in future she shouldn't be so optimistic, that when some cad, some bastard called her name, she shouldn't appear so open. That she was opening herself for hurt.

'I do have an appointment today but if I can swing it with Marshall, perhaps we could have dinner tonight.'

She shouldn't be nodding. Iosef winced. She should be telling him she'd get back to him about dinner, or pulling out a bleeping mobile, not smiling and waving and wearing her heart on her sleeve as he drove off.

Not being Annie.

'Where did you say we're going?'

Sinking back into her seat, Annie looked out of the window as his sleek car silently gobbled up the miles, the city a golden glint in the rear-view mirror as the sun set over the bay.

'I know a really nice restaurant—right on the water. It's a bit of a drive, but worth it.'

It was.

Tucked away in a secluded cove, the restaurant sat on the end of a pier, the food so fresh Annie half expected to look out and see the chef casting his line. But it wasn't the food or romantic surroundings that made the night special—it was the company.

Sharing a sumptuous seafood platter, washed down with icy glasses of tonic water with dashes of lime, they chatted easily.

'The experience was good, I guess.' Iosef shrugged when she asked about his work in Russia. 'I learnt to think for myself—make the best use of the facilities available.'

'Is that why you don't like asking for help?'

'I guess,' he answered, then shook his head. 'I know if I do it myself that it's done…' His voice trailed off and Annie smiled.

'You're a control freak.'

'No!' He actually smiled back at her rather bold statement.

'You need to delegate.' Annie dipped a

massive tiger prawn in citrus mayonnaise. 'Or you'll burn out.'

'If I was ever going to burn out, I think it would have happened in Russia. As busy as it can be here, the facilities are good and there is always back-up.'

'Would you go back?'

'Maybe. I miss the kids.' He must have seen her frown, must have seen her eyes start just a touch. After all, involvement with children was one of the few things that wasn't demanded from a trauma specialist.

'The kids?' Annie repeated, and he actually laughed.

'There is no ex-Mrs Kolovsky. In Russia I volunteered on my days off at the detsky doms—children's homes,' he translated.

'As a doctor?'

'Absolutely—these children have a lot of physiological problems as well as psychological ones. There's always a lot to be done. Still, it was the right time to come back.'

'Because of your father?' She watched his face stiffen, watched his hand pause for a fraction as he raised his glass to his lips, but he quickly righted himself, answering her with a dismissive shrug and a casual voice that Annie was sure was false. 'I guess—there are a lot of changes happening at the moment. And Levander was getting married. My father wanted to discuss what would happen with the business. Probably Aleksi will take over.'

'How come Levander isn't?' Annie pushed. 'I thought he was the eldest.'

'He doesn't want it,' Iosef answered tightly, 'and I can't say I blame him. Anyway, enough about my family…'

'Please, no!' Annie groaned. 'You really don't want to know about mine.'

Actually, he hadn't been about to ask, was just trying to drop the subject of his own family, but she had him curious now.

'Do you have brothers and sisters?'

'Two sisters,' Annie groaned, 'both perfect!'

'Perfect?'

'Perfect!' Annie confirmed glumly. 'Bianca's a lawyer and Jennifer trained as a journalist and is now…' she pulled a little face '…a senior political media advisor.'

'Heavy title.'

'Not a heavy woman, though,' Annie sighed. 'They're both tiny, both gorgeous, both thoroughly together and focused and, unlike me, neither have given my parents a single moment of worry.'

'Of course not.' Iosef grinned. 'They were too busy concentrating on their studies and careers.'

'Nice try.' Annie gave a resigned smile. 'They're also both extremely happily married, have perfectly tidy houses and occasionally pop out beautiful, contented babies with absolute ease and return to work six weeks later!'

He laughed, actually threw his head back and laughed—it was the first time she'd seen or heard him laugh and it gave her a tiny thrill to know it was down to her.

'You have a great career.'

'Not according to my parents. They have a similar view of nurses as you seem to.'

'My issues are with myself, not my colleagues,' Iosef said. 'They didn't like the idea of you nursing?'

'I come from a long line of high achievers.' Annie gave a tight shrug. 'They seem to think I could have done better.'

'I know how you feel.' He nodded as she blinked her doubt—positive that he didn't know. 'My parents were both horrified when I told them I wanted to study medicine.'

'Really?' Annie frowned.

'Really,' Iosef confirmed.

'But why? Any parent would be delighted.'

'Do you know what my mother said?' He leant forward just a touch, and as she did so too she felt as if she were leaning into his world just a little bit, as if she was actually being let in. 'Her exact words—in Russian, mind you—were, "Why would you want to be a doctor, Iosef? There's no real money in medicine."'

'We're both black sheep, I guess.' Annie laughed—she'd never expected him to understand. Never expected that someone as dashing and successful as Iosef could even fathom where she was coming from, let alone have walked along a similar road. 'Families are complicated,' Annie added, and felt her heart thud in her chest as his expression was suddenly solemn.

'My family has always been difficult—and never more so than now…' Eyes that had been holding hers comfortably as they spoke were darting now. 'Things really are incredibly complicated for me at the moment.'

'Because of your father?'

'Because of many things.'

'Such as?' Till then it had all been going so well, like coming in from the cold and warming your hands over the fire, just this lovely glow surrounding them. But she'd got too close. Almost immediately she realised she'd crossed some line, saw the tiny shake of his head, and though she braced herself for pain, when it came it was way more brutal than she'd expected. 'I can't see you, Annie. What I said last night about not being available for a relationship—I meant it.'

She didn't know how to take it. She'd thought tonight had gone so well, but suddenly she felt as if she'd failed whatever test he'd just put her through, as if he'd decided to give her a second go and still she wasn't quite up to scratch. But unlike this morning she was not going to roll over and just accept it.

'I think it's a bit early to be using the word *relationship.*'

'Dating, then?' Iosef offered. 'It's really not possible right now. As I said, things are just so complicated for me at the moment—I don't see that it could work.'

Staring at him across the table, recalling last night—not just the love-making, the before, during and after, the laughter, the tenderness, the *everything*—Annie couldn't pretend not to care.

'Why are you here, then, Iosef? If a one-night

stand was all you wanted, why did you ask me out to dinner tonight?'

'Because…' He closed his eyes, held the bridge of his nose in his fingers for a second as he attempted to come up with a suitable answer, only he couldn't. And the only response Annie could come up with on his behalf wasn't very flattering—wasn't flattering at all.

'Because you felt sorry for me? Thought that after such a good shag, the least you could do was buy me dinner?'

'Don't be crude.' He shook his head at her description, yet he didn't say or do anything to refute it.

'I feel crude.' Her eyes flashed with a mixture of anger and tears. 'I feel stupid, too. I thought you asked me here because you wanted to see me again, not to tell me that you couldn't. You could have done that when you dropped me off this morning.'

She wasn't making this easy.

Iosef closed his eyes and dragged in air as he corrected himself.

He wasn't finding this easy, though with his track record he should—after all, he was more than used to tears and protests when a relationship inevitably ended, and rather too used to letting a woman down the morning after. Hell, he'd spelt out last night that he wasn't available—had made himself very clear that a relationship now was out of the question.

Out of the question.

He reinforced those words as he paid the bill and they walked to the car.

Said it over and over to himself as they bristled in silence on the horribly long drive home.

Said it again as he dropped her off at her flat, trying to stare fixedly ahead as she stumbled up the drive, wishing she'd just find her keys and get the hell inside.

What the hell had he been thinking?

Tonight he'd told her things that he hadn't even thought about let alone discussed with another person. She was so easy to talk to…

Too easy to talk to!

The last thing he needed right now was a dizzy, emotional woman like Annie... As she finally entered the house he gunned the engine and pulled out.

She was far from discreet—she'd be blushing and dropping things and sulking if he tried to ignore her. The whole department could tell her mood from the second she either bounced or slumped in the door at the start of her shift—hell, he'd wager she'd had her period last week.

As the lights conspired against him and he pulled up at the red light, Iosef tapped out a restless silent tune on his leather-covered steering-wheel.

Annie Jameson was... He tried to think of a suitable word, one that he could use like a mantra to warn himself off—gullible, susceptible, dizzy...adorable!

Performing a thoroughly illegal U-turn, Iosef muttered a curse at the car hooting at him but cursed himself more.

What the hell was he doing?

Even as he walked up her path, even as he rang her doorbell, the question raged loudly, but one look at her tear-stained face as the door opened, hearing the sob on her lips at the sight of him, silenced, at least for a little while, the doubts about the foolishness of his ways.

'We have to keep things quiet.' He was holding her in his arms, kissing away her tears. 'No one at work must know—it would just make things incredibly awkward.'

'I know.' He could feel her head frantically nodding against his chest.

'I can't see you much at the moment—what with my father being so ill and everything, my time is taken up…'

'I understand!'

Trusting eyes looked up at him and he felt like the biggest swine in the world.

He even opened his mouth to tell her the truth— but at the last second thought better of it and went instead for the infinitely more pleasurable option.

Losing himself in her kiss.

CHAPTER NINE

'IT MIGHT sting a little bit…' Annie tried to be gentle as she cleaned up the teenage boy's hands, not that he seemed to care particularly. He just stared up at the ceiling as she had when it had been her turn, only, unlike her, he didn't try to make conversation. 'Can you tell me what happened, Mark?'

'Answer the question, Mark!' Mr Taylor, his father, barked.

'I've already told you—I fell.'

Right. And he'd bounced so hard when he'd hit the ground he'd *then* landed on the other side of his body and managed to catch his knuckles on his teeth in the process.

'Afternoon!' Iosef introduced himself to Mark and his parents before running a cursory eye over the casualty card and the more obvious wounds, and then addressed his patient.

'It says here that you fell.'

'I did.'

'Of course he didn't fall,' snapped Mr Taylor, but for the moment Iosef ignored him.

'I am going to examine you if that's OK, Mark.' He turned to the parents. 'Could I ask you to step outside?'

'We'd rather stay here.' Mrs Taylor gave a tight smile. 'We'd like to see what's going on for ourselves.'

'At fifteen years old, it may be uncomfortable for Mark to have his parents present while he is examined.'

'At fifteen years old,' Mr Taylor responded tersely, 'he's still legally a child and we'd rather stay.'

'OK.' Surprisingly for Iosef he didn't argue the point and Annie frowned just a touch as he pulled on a pair of gloves and performed a comprehensive examination. He did his best to keep

Mark covered as he probed his chest and abdomen then rolled him over and checked some rather large bruises on his back, performed a neurological examination then carefully checked a nasty laceration on his scalp.

'This will need suturing,' Iosef said, though more to himself, then spoke to his patient. 'Is there anywhere I haven't examined that you're hurting, anything else that happened when you fell?'

'He didn't fall,' Mr Taylor snarled. 'So can we all stop playing along with his lies? We want to know what's going on with him. Today isn't the first problem we've had. He's hardly ever at school, has been coming home at all hours and when he is home is shut in his room. Heaven only knows what he's on, whether it's drugs or alcohol—'

'OK,' Iosef interrupted. 'Clearly there are things that need to be discussed so could I now ask again that you excuse us so that I can talk to your son?'

'And I'm telling you again that we want to hear what he has to say!' Mr Taylor barked. 'You haven't even asked him if he's taken anything.'

'Mark.' Iosef turned briefly to his patient. 'Have you taken anything?'

'No.'

'That's not asking him.' Mr Taylor's face was twisted with rage and Annie watched as Mark just closed his eyes. 'As if he's going to just admit it!'

'So what do you suggest I do?' Iosef asked.

'We have to get to the bottom of this,' Mrs Taylor said.

'I agree—but I don't think is likely to happen with you in the room,' Iosef answered, and his voice was still calm and easy. 'I think there is more chance of Mark talking to me without you present.'

'Well, if we do leave we want to know everything that's said. Legally you can't—'

'Annie…' Iosef spoke over Mr Taylor. 'Are there any beds in the obs ward?'

She shook her head. 'Not for a couple of hours. Hopefully the tendon repair will be leaving around six.'

'Do you know if there are beds on the children's ward?'

'I'll check,' Annie answered. Mark was at that difficult age where he really couldn't be crammed in beside a three-year-old.

'Thanks.' He turned to Mr and Mrs Taylor. 'He needs to be sutured, and given you are concerned there may be drugs or alcohol involved, and also that he has some renal tenderness, I'd like your son to be admitted overnight for observation. Annie, could we also check his urine for any blood, please?'

'And drugs!' Mr Taylor demanded, at which Iosef gave an ironic smile and spoke to Annie.

'Forget the obs ward—I'll go and ring the paediatricians.'

'That's it.' Mr Taylor was incensed as Iosef turned to leave.

'The paediatricians will discuss your son's care with you and whether to do a drug screen—and naturally a social worker will—'

'You're just going to leave! We just said he could talk to you.'

'Mr Taylor.' Still his voice was calm, yet

somehow it overrode the angry one. 'I have worked with many teenagers and I have dealt with many who are in serious trouble. Confidentiality is a very difficult area. Now, I absolutely agree with your concerns about your son's welfare and I understand that there are things you, no doubt, want and need to know. Your son presents to me as a young man who is in trouble, a young man, who like many, cannot, for whatever reason, talk openly with his parents. Me talking to Mark alone and having then to relay *everything* to you is, I believe, a pointless exercise. My speciality is emergency medicine— the paediatricians and the child psychologist are far more qualified to deal with family matters.' He glanced at the casualty card. 'In a few weeks your son will be old enough and hopefully well enough to get the confidential advice and care he needs.'

And even if he was out of the cubicle now, he wasn't washing his hands of the matter. In fact, by having Mark admitted to the paediatric ward as opposed to Obs, he was actually offering the family more care, only somehow it didn't feel like it. He was so direct, so absolutely open in what he was saying and respectful to Mark that everyone present knew that even if he had to keep it short and sweet, the care they could get from this doctor would probably be the best start for them all.

'Can you see where we're coming from?' Mr Taylor asked. 'We want to help him and unless we know what's going on, we can't. How do we know that you'll say the right thing?'

'You don't.' Iosef didn't even blink. 'Though, given my job, given that I am used to dealing with this age group and the problems they face, you can feel fairly safe that I won't make things worse.

'Let me at least *try* to talk with your son. Unless someone does that—unless he opens up to someone—then there can be nothing to tell.' For the longest time he looked at Mr Taylor. 'I understand that I am asking you to sign a contract without reading it. I am asking you to trust me with the most precious thing in your life—with not much guarantee. We can discuss legalities for longer than anyone has time for but right now I believe it is in everyone's best interests to find out what is going on with your son.'

'Talk to him, Mark.' Mr Taylor gave a terse nod.

'Annie.' Iosef gave her a polite smile. 'Could you show Mr and Mrs Taylor to an interview room, please?'

He was, of course, booting her out too, Annie realized, only it didn't irk as it had before, and she didn't feel as if she was being dismissed, was just curious as to what he would say to the young man, curious as to how he would relay it to the parents, but more than that she was curious that a man so aloof and so cutting at times could somehow be the most caring and perceptive of them all.

For all she knew of him, for all the time she spent with him, it was as if she'd merely scratched the surface there was layer after layer to this complicated man that she wanted to explore, yet at every turn he thwarted her.

Gave her all his attention when they were alone together but only a little piece of his mind.

There was no trouble with anyone picking up on them at work—no one could possibly have guessed there was anything between them.

He was just as cool with her.

Just as dismissive.

Though he did now call her Annie.

He more than made up for it when they saw each other—whisking her away for a romantic midweek break, giving her a piece of jewellery that would surely have covered a year's rent— somehow it wasn't enough.

Wasn't enough to ease the growing disquiet that gnawed away at her, that wouldn't hush when she scolded herself that she was being greedy, wanting too much too soon.

Wanting pieces of Iosef that he didn't seem ready or willing to give.

It was a funny shift—lots of lulls and no one particularly critical.

George was flicking through holiday brochures

and Annie sat nibbling on a bar of chocolate, waiting for the place to get busy.

'Tell me if the boss comes.' George looked up. 'He wouldn't be too impressed with me sitting here, looking at these.'

'Iosef wouldn't care about that and anyway…' Annie gave a dismissive shrug '…I'm over pretending to look busy. We work more than hard enough when it's needed.'

'You don't know him,' George said, and Annie could only inwardly agree. 'He tells me I should be doing things, that there's plenty to do, then as soon as I go to do it he's already there. He's got no patience—his way is best.'

'I think he's just used to working on his own,' Annie attempted.

'Well, this is a teaching hospital. Take that kid he's talking to now. Why couldn't I have dealt with that?'

'That one's actually a bit complicated.' Annie nibbled on her bottom lip. 'It's turned out to be more serious than it looks.'

'I know that,' George moaned. 'I spoke to the dad when the kid was first brought in, I said I'd talk to his son and find out what was going on. Then Dr Control Freak marches in and decides it's more appropriate if someone more senior deals with this patient and family.'

She could see both sides—she truly could.

George wanted experience.

Iosef could do it better.

But George couldn't get the experience if Iosef didn't let him make a few mistakes.

But these were people's lives they were dealing with.

'You just wait…' There was no stopping George now as he angrily turned the pages. 'I'll be called into his office for a lecture tomorrow so I can see hear how marvellously he handled things. I may as well be home, reading a medical textbook!'

'George!' A curt voice had them both jumping. 'Haven't you got something better to do than read holiday brochures?'

'Oh, sorry!' George attempted sarcasm. 'I forgot to do the dishes in the staffroom.'

'What are you smiling at?' Iosef asked Annie as George marched off.

'Him.' She shrugged. 'You.'

'He's annoyed because I didn't let him talk to Mark or his family.'

'To any family,' Annie pointed out, and she *was* actually talking to him as she would any colleague. 'Or to too many patients either—well, not the really sick ones.'

'I make those decisions.'

'I know you do.' Annie smiled. 'I just deal with the fallout.'

'Now, if you've finished your chocolate break, could you come with me, please, to speak to the family? I want the nursing staff to know what's going on—and I really have to go soon.'

As they headed for the interview room, he changed his mind, did a quick about-turn and tapped on the staffroom door and asked George to come with them.

The tense, angry people Annie had left in there were now just two weary, utterly terrified parents waiting to hear what the doctor had to say.

'I have spoken at length with your son.' Iosef sat down and went straight to a rather surprising point. 'He has, in fact, agreed that I tell you all that was said—which makes things a lot easier for everyone. Now, there is some news that will not be good and there is some news that is probably not as bad as you fear.'

'And he's really OK with you talking to us?' Mr Taylor blinked. 'How on earth did you get him to agree to that?'

'I told your son he had many choices—he could ignore the help or he could get everything out in the open now and once everyone has calmed down, you deal with it all together. The reason I wanted to treat your son, I have worked with many, many trouble teenagers—in an orphanage in Russia.' Annie's gaze flicked to George who sort of gave a half-smile. 'But,' Iosef continued, 'as experienced as I am with this age group and the troubles that they get themselves into, dealing with the family unit is somewhat uncharted waters for me. As I explained to him, more often than not I did not have the luxury of children with parents who were cross or did not understand—because there were no parents— so I hope that by telling him he should try to trust that you will prove me right.' He sort of eye-balled them till they nodded.

'Apparently there are parent-teacher interviews in two weeks' time. You are going to find out that your son has fallen very behind with his maths homework and he has, in fact, intercepted two letters from the school.'

'But he's good at maths.' Mr Taylor shook his head as his wife put her hand on his arm to silence him. 'Go on.'

'Because he was worried what the teacher would say, he has been avoiding lessons and spending his time at the park—and he recently started smoking marijuana.' Their faces were as white as chalk as the news sank in, then they finally nodded and Annie could actually see them brace themselves for whatever was coming next. 'This morning he owed some children some money. Though he didn't want to go to the park, he couldn't go to school either.'

'And he couldn't tell us...' Mrs Taylor was crying now.

'So, when he didn't have the money, he got a beating.'

'What else?' Mr Taylor asked. 'What else is he taking?'

'I think he may have had some beer, but that is it.'

'No other drugs.'

'I don't think so.' Iosef stared at them for a long time, his face growing more serious as their relief started to show. 'Marijuana can lead to depression. It is also linked with schizophrenia, and it is not something to be relaxed about.'

'Of course not,' Mr Taylor said. 'But we honestly thought—well, I don't know what we thought.'

'I would say that the best thing that happened

to your son and to your family was that he got beaten up and ended up in here today. The stress of this parent-teacher interview coming up has been huge for him and he has dealt with it by self-medicating and lying and getting himself in deeper at every turn.'

'He could have just spoken to us,' Mrs Taylor cried again. 'Come and told us what was going on, right at the start. We could have got him a tutor….'

'He felt he couldn't talk to you.'

'But if he'd just come to us…'

'He felt he couldn't.' Iosef said again. 'That is how he felt. Now, my concern is that this will quickly be sorted out. He will be admitted and perhaps followed up with a counsellor. You in turn will deal with the school and after a few difficult weeks things will seem much better. However, when something goes wrong in his life again—which, naturally, it will—I would expect that this is how he will deal with it. Unless…'

'Unless what?'

'You work together and you all get proper help to open the lines of communication and work to keep them open. This will hopefully be addressed on the children's ward, but I cannot recommend strongly enough that you get family counseling. More than that, make sure you see someone good and *then* listen to what they say.'

'Can you recommend anyone?' Mr Taylor asked. 'We're happy to go privately.'

'Actually, I can recommend someone I think would be good for Mark.' He turned to Annie and pulled out his keys. 'Can you get my jacket and wallet from the office? I have a business card. I know this man from university and I often rang him for advice when I was in Russia. He is pretty direct, though.'

'Seems like we need it.'

'Don't beat yourself up over this,' Annie heard Iosef say as she slipped out, and as she walked through the department and glanced up at a clock that showed Iosef should have been home hours ago, she was really glad that he'd stayed.

Emergency contained such an eclectic mix of patients and problems and even though Mark's problem didn't seem that serious, to Iosef it had been. He had been treated just as thoroughly as a critically injured patient. Unlocking his office and stepping inside, Annie concluded Iosef may not have saved a life tonight but he'd certainly given someone a very good chance of turning theirs around.

And with a little nudge from Annie he'd taught George an awful lot, too.

His office was in darkness, but his computer provided enough light for Annie not to turn the overhead one on. She just waltzed over and picked up his jacket.

One file lay on his desk. *Mickey Baker's.*

The meanie *still* had his notes—he had just been taunting her with them. A smile on her face, she started to go and jumped slightly as the mobile phone on his desk lit up and vibrated into life.

She wasn't snooping but she felt like an

intruder, especially when she read the name that popped onto the screen of his phone. Her tongue stuck to the roof of her mouth and she headed for the door.

Candy.

'Thanks.' He was back at the nurses' station, and glanced up as she handed him his jacket and keys and he fished out his wallet. 'Could you give them this card for me? I can't risk getting caught up again—I'm already running terribly late.'

'For what?'

Would she have asked anyone else that question? Annie wondered as she swore she saw his jaw tighten a fraction. Was that bringing things to work, or just two colleagues talking? She honestly didn't know.

'Just late getting off—I should have been out of here two hours ago. I'd better go.'

'You left your computer on in your office,' Annie reminded him. 'And your phone.'

'Thanks.' He checked that no one was around

and for the first time at work he spoke to her intimately. 'Are you OK?'

'Of course I am.'

'I'll give you a call a bit later when your shift's finished—maybe I can drop by…'

'I'm really tired, actually.'

'I'm not asking to be entertained.'

'I really just want to go home, have a bath and go to bed.' Which was a rather long way of saying she would prefer it if he didn't come over.

And he couldn't really push for answers when he refused to let her ask questions, Annie realised as he headed back to his office, wondering if when he picked up his phone he might work out what was upsetting her, wondering if he'd even give it a second thought.

The Taylors were actually talking as she entered—OK, not sitting around gossiping like old friends exactly, but there was a conversation taking place and even though Mark looked like he'd been crying, he looked a whole lot less tense than he had.

'Dr Kolovsky asked me to give you this.' Annie handed Mr Taylor the card. 'He's sorry not to pass it on himself, but he had to go.'

'That's quite all right. I'm aware he stayed behind to help us. I've told him how grateful we are to him for his directness and no-nonsense approach, but if you can pass our thanks on to him again when you see him, that would be appreciated.'

'I will.'

'Look at me!' George called from the mini-theatre as she walked past, washing his hands at the sink and making her laugh. 'Iosef's actually gone home and left me Mark to suture.'

'See!' Annie said. 'He does trust you after all.'

'Nice try at boosting my ego.' George grinned as he put in the boot. 'But I think a certain ex-supermodel might have had some small part in his haste to get out of here tonight.'

Strange, Annie reflected later as she lay in the bath, barely making a ripple, her body quite still and her mind curiously quiet. For someone who insisted on straight talking, who seemed utterly unabashed by confrontation, for someone who could so easily discuss other people's issues, he certainly wasn't good at talking about himself.

Quickly Annie heaved herself out of the bath. Her mind was starting to race now, the image of the blue screen of his phone flashing before her eyes, that name branded on her brain, but, pulling out the plug, wrapping herself in a towel, Annie refused to go there.

Iosef had told her she had nothing to worry about with Candy. He'd told her that things would be difficult for the next few weeks with his father so ill.

She made herself a cup of soup, climbed into bed with a really good book, set her alarm and determinedly tried not to think about it.

For about ten seconds!

Why didn't they ever go out!'

Why did it have to be like some sort of covert operation just to have a private conversation at work?

Draining her cup, Annie turned back to her book and made it to the end of page two.

Just because Candy had rung him this evening, it didn't mean he was dashing off to see her. And he'd hardly been dashing off—his shift should have ended two hours before he'd left.

Turning off the light, she gave up.

Gave up trying to convince herself she knew the answers and gave up asking herself questions.

It was just so much easier to believe him.

CHAPTER TEN

'Do you think anyone at work knows?' Melanie asked, sitting at Annie's laden dressing-table and dragging ceramic hair straighteners through her hair.

'Knows what?' Annie said nervously.

'About me and George, of course.'

'I'm not sure,' Annie lied, buzzing her latest contraption along her shins and biting on her lip as yet another guaranteed pain-free hair removal system failed to deliver. 'Though you two don't exactly try to keep it quiet!'

'Why would we?' Melanie blinked at Annie in the mirror. 'I mean, we're not exactly broadcasting the fact that we're a couple, but there's no crime against it. Why on earth would we keep it quiet?'

'I don't know.' Annie shrugged. 'I guess if you break up, things could get awkward…'

'Oh, please!' Melanie rolled her eyes. 'As if there aren't half a million exes working side by side at the hospital. I'm sure we could manage to remain civil if we ever broke up!'

'I guess,' Annie said casually, but Melanie's words were biting. Why *did* Iosef insist on keeping thing things so secret? Why couldn't she be sitting on the bed, gossiping to Melanie about the man who made her heart flip? 'But some people just like to keep their work and personal lives separate, I suppose.' Only Melanie wasn't listening. Bored with doing her hair, now she was trying on lipstick as she rattled on about the fabulous George!

'He's so impulsive. We were at the shops the other day, just to grab some supplies, and next thing I know we're in a travel agent's. He wants to go to Queensland for a long weekend! I'm going to ask Cheryl if I can swap my days off.'

'Sounds great!'

'I know.' Melanie giggled. 'You know, he's fantastic—I mean, I know he's not spectacular to look at…'

'He's lovely!' Annie wailed.

'I know he is,' Melanie countered, 'but…' She gave a shrug. 'I can be me with him. Imagine being that Candy.'

'Candy?' Annie tried to sound casual, grateful she could concentrate on the diversion of her legs and didn't have to meet her friend's eyes.

'Iosef's girlfriend,' Melanie carried on. 'Imagine trying to hold onto *that*!'

'I don't think they're together any more,' Annie attempted. 'I mean, I haven't seen her around lately.'

'She's probably at a health farm.' Melanie giggled again. 'Or having a few hundred units of line fillers and Botox squeezed into her face so she can stay gorgeous for him!'

'I don't think Iosef's like that.' The temptation to talk about him was too much, the need for insight, even if it was misguided, too much to pass up. 'He's nothing like the rest of them. He's worked in Russia for the last few years and did a lot of voluntary work, too—with troubled kids. I really don't think he's that superficial—he just doesn't seem into all that, if you ask me. I'm sure he wouldn't give two hoots what a woman looked like!'

'Please!' Melanie was really laughing now. 'You *know* that's utter bilge. Oh, we can all say the PC things, that looks don't matter, etc., but I defy any woman to date a guy like Iosef Kolovsky and *not* be intimidated by all the super-models that have come and gone. I mean, he's beautiful to look at and everything, but give me George any day. Who needs that sort of pressure?' Seeing Annie's agonised expression, her voice trailed off. 'Hey, are you OK, Annie? Did I say something wrong?'

'No, it's just this stupid shaving thing.' Annie forced a smile but struggled to hold it. 'It really hurts.'

'You get used to it apparently.' Melanie

shrugged, picking up her bag and dousing herself with Annie's scent before dashing off to spend the rest of the night with George. 'Why don't you just wait a couple of weeks and get them waxed?'

Because she didn't *have* a couple of weeks—at any time Iosef could appear. And often did.

He kept the most peculiar hours, almost constantly on call, not just for work but with his father's death approaching, his mother, Nina, was constantly ringing, questioning Ivan's treatments, his medications, and Annie understood if sometimes it wasn't till after midnight that he appeared or on occasion had to go soon after getting there.

Melanie was right, Annie thought darkly as her phone bleeped loudly in her bag. When Iosef was coming round she would dash to the bathroom to brush her teeth then back to the bedroom to squirt on perfume. As much as she was loath to admit it—never, not once, had he made a negative comment on her appearance—the pressure *was* on. Over and over he told her she looked fantastic, felt fantastic, smelt fantastic, tasted fantastic—but Annie was finding *that* a pressure in itself!

What happened if he called round and she wasn't looking, feeling, smelling and tasting fantastic? Her pink, flannelette, cheeky-monkey pyjamas had been dumped in favour of a flimsy sarong, every pair of granny knickers she owned had been replaced by an overdraft-funded selection of lacy bras and panties, her skin was permanently defuzzed and moisturized, and that was before she squeezed in nails, hair and, oh, yes, thanks to some freaky, obsessive compulsive perfect housewife show she'd watched, her bed was now decked out in starched white linen, which meant constant trips to the laundry.

'Hey!' He gave a tired smile as he stood in her doorway. 'Sorry it's so late. I got caught up.'

'No problem. Melanie was just here.' She moved to let him in. 'How's your dad?'

'Don't ask!' He didn't say it nastily, more wearily, sitting on the sofa and running a tired hand over his face. 'I've had one of those nights—you know…'

Only she didn't know because he didn't tell her, and she didn't push because he looked awful—beautiful but awful all at the same time. His exquisite features, more chiselled somehow, dark smudges under his eyes, as if he'd suddenly lost weight or just got over flu or something. Annie could actually *feel* the great weariness that emanated from him. He gave a tight smile as his phone started trilling and with a small eye roll he answered it.

'Hi, Levander.' That was the one in England, Annie registered, which meant he wouldn't be talking long. But clearly a little thing like the cost of an international call to a mobile phone didn't matter a hoot to the Kolovskys. Clearly, because forty minutes later, having left Iosef to it long ago, she was lying on top of the bed, staring up at the ceiling, listening without a clue as to what was being said as he spoke to his brother in Russian from the lounge.

Just what had he come here for? He didn't want to talk to her. She wasn't allowed to ask what was going on. Was it really just sex that he wanted from her?

'Sorry I took so long…' He sat on the edge of the bed and took her reluctant hand, playing with her fingers as she still stared at the ceiling. 'I don't know whether to tell him to come now for my father, or if it's too soon…'

'Does it matter?' Finally she looked at him. 'If he comes now, maybe he can have a bit of quality time with your dad before…' She gave a tiny little swallow, forced herself to go on and willed him not to push her out. 'I mean, your dad can meet his grandson and get to hold him.' She might just as well have been speaking in Urdu or Japanese because he closed his eyes at her efforts, making it very clear that either she didn't get it, or he simply didn't understand, and as he lay on the bed beside her, buried his head in her neck, for the first time she wanted to reject him—didn't want to sleep with someone who on every other level was pulling away from her.

But again she'd misread him.

'I wish this was over…' He groaned out the words, pulled her in tightly as he gave her a shocking glimpse of what was going on in his head. 'Don't give up on me yet, Annie.'

He was asleep before he'd even finished talking, a deep sleep where he held her fiercely all night, an exhausted sleep where there was no energy to even undress, and if it was the least sexual they'd ever been, somehow it was the most intimate.

But that was scary for Annie, too.

Scary, because she didn't want to give up on them either, didn't want to ask the questions that would inevitably end it, didn't want to face the truth.

But on a deeper level she knew she had to.

'What are you going to do with your day off?'

His body, naked now, was pressed behind her,

warm hands holding her, sleepy voices enjoying that delicious time fifteen minutes *after* the alarm clock had gone off.

'I'll think of something.' Annie yawned, hoping she sounded mysterious, choosing *not* to tell him that she was getting yet another spray tan, a pedicure and her hair blow-dried straight again— because if the tan faded, then so to might they.

She knew it was shallow—loathed the effort she put in to keep him—but the first night they'd made love she'd been as groomed as she'd ever been. Rolling over, she stared at him, didn't say a word, just stared at the most beautiful man who had just made spectacular, lazy morning love to her, and told herself it was worth it.

'What are you thinking?'

'That you're beautiful…' It was the most honest she'd ever been with him.

'Same.'

As he climbed out of bed she already missed him. That hint of an accent, the sheer joy of being with him just spun her out. Lying in his arms, she felt she belonged, but the second he left she knew she didn't. He was so much more than some diamond in the rough she'd discovered—it was like finding a Fabergé egg in the cupboard under the sink, each stroke of her finger revealing something too precious to keep—something that she knew didn't really belong to her. Devotion was dangerous, blurred the rules and botched all boundaries…

Made excuses when there should be none.

'Here…' He brought her coffee and the paper as she lay there fitfully thinking, and it was easier to sit up and take a sip of her drink and read the paper than deal with all that was on her mind. 'I don't think I can come over tonight, but tomorrow…'

'I want to see that.' Flicking from her horoscope to the movie guide, Annie tapped at an advertisement. 'It sounds really good.'

'Why don't you?' Iosef asked, giving the completely wrong reaction. 'I'm not coming tonight and I can remember Melanie saying something about wanting to see it.'

She didn't want to go to the movies with Melanie—well, she did, but not *this* movie. Growing more unsettled by the second, she flicked through the paper as he dressed, gazing unseeingly at the words until her eye was caught not by a headline but by a photo, Iosef and his family walking out of a plush restaurant, her stomach knotting as she saw his hand firmly linked in Candy's.

House of Turmoil.

The headline gave a teasing taste of what was to come. Her mind worked ten to the dozen as Iosef chatted unwittingly on while he dressed. Annie silently read about the growing turmoil reported to be within the House of Kolovsky— the obvious declining health of its founder, the public and business world's growing fascination with who would be named heir and whether or not the hugely successful empire could be sustained without the maverick personality of Ivan Kolovsky. And it would have been fascinating if her heart wasn't thumping so loudly in her chest, if a picture of the man in her room hadn't been plastered above the article, holding hands with his girlfriend…

'There's a piece about your family in here!' Somehow she kept her voice light, watched as his hands paused for just a second on the way to pick up his wallet from the bedside table.

'There's always something about my family in the newspaper.'

'It talks about you!' She watched as he gave a surly shrug. 'It says that with Levander in the UK and Aleksi back in Australia, he's the son most likely to take over, especially given Annika is a designer and you—'

'I have no interest in hearing or reading some journalist who has no idea, spouting what he thinks he knows about my family!' Iosef interrupted.

'There's a photo here, too.' Annie forced herself to look at him, her throat tightening as he turned to go, giving the paper a very cursory glance. 'You're holding hands with Candy.'

'So?'

'So…' Annie swallowed. 'What the hell are you doing holding hands with her when—?'

'It's an old photo,' Iosef interrupted. 'They've used a library photo. Next week it will be someone I dated in high school. You are going to have to get used to seeing me in the paper, you are going to have to get used to not believing everything you read.'

His goodbye kiss was so haphazard it barely grazed her cheek and though it couldn't be classed as a row, couldn't even be classed as a disagreement, as the front door closed behind him, as she heard his car purr into life and leave, her heart was hammering as if they'd had the most vile of confrontations.

They *had* had the most vile of confrontations, Annie realised, running a shaky hand through her hair, suddenly glad he couldn't make it tonight, suddenly glad that she could put off till tomorrow what should have been done not just today but weeks ago.

She *didn't* believe everything she read, but she

knew what she'd seen—and it wasn't the dart of his eyes that had her convinced he had been lying, hadn't been the set of his lips as he'd tried to tell her otherwise... The truth was much simpler than that.

Irrefutable, actually.

Staring down at the photo, his image blurred on the page, only not enough to hide the truth because unless Iosef made a habit of slashing his cheek two inches beneath his right eye with a razor on a regular basis, he was lying.

Hurling the paper against the wall, Annie swore she'd accept no excuses, swore that the next time they were alone she'd confront him with what she now knew...

The first morning they'd made love, he'd climbed out of bed and gone to *her*.

CHAPTER ELEVEN

'WHAT do you mean, the bed's not made?' The phone was hot in his hands as he loudly demanded that any red tape be swiftly cut. 'No, I've already listened to how busy you are on the ward—now it's your turn to listen to me! In between resuscitating a four-year-old and trying to get this thirty-nine-year-old terminally ill woman out of pain, I have had to sit on this phone, trying to find a single room for her. And when I finally get one, when I finally tell her family that she will soon be in a private bed and more comfortable, you tell me that you are *still* waiting for the domestic staff to come and make it.'

Stuffing syringes into a drawer and tearing up

alcohol swabs, Annie and Jackie shared a wide-eyed glance as Iosef continued angrily.

'No—you listen! If you do not ring me back in the next five minutes to tell me that you are ready for her, I will bring her up myself and *I'll* make the bed!' He didn't even hang up, just tossed the phone in the vague direction of the wall as he muttered something in Russian that certainly didn't sound too complimentary.

'Thirty-nine!' He finally said to Jackie. 'Thirty-bloody-nine—and she has to put off dying comfortably to wait on someone to come and make a bed!'

'You know it's not that straightforward,' Jackie said. 'I'll ring the nursing co-ordinator and try to speed things along.'

'I've done that,' Iosef retorted. 'And still nothing has been done.'

'Well maybe if a consultant rings, she'll listen.'

'That's a very good point.' Iosef glanced up meaningfully at her.

'I hardly think this is the place to discuss it.'

'I want the consultant's position. I have no issues with discussing it in front of anyone.' Iosef shrugged. He clearly had no issues with confrontation or negotiation either. 'I have made my feelings very clear since the day I arrived here.'

'You've certainly done that!' Jackie responded, but her voice trailed off as the woman's anxious husband appeared.

'Any news on when she can get to the ward, Doctor? I'm sorry to keep asking, it's just the kids are getting restless and that young guy in the next cubicle keeps swearing and waking her…'

'We're going to move your wife to the obs ward here—right now it's empty and will be a lot more comfortable and peaceful.' Annie didn't dare look at Jackie's expression as he snapped his fingers at Beth to get a move on and get things under way. The obs ward was Jackie's baby, and for Iosef to open it up and at the same time effectively close it, without even discussing it with her, was just so not the way things were done.

Not that it stopped him.

'No further patients are to be admitted to Obs until Mrs Lucas is moved up to the ward—and when she is moved just do a bed swap. She is not to be transferred to a bed twice. Ring me if the ward kicks up about it, and you are to buzz me if she needs anything—anything at all.'

'Thanks, Doctor.' Mr Lucas gave a tearful nod of appreciation. 'It means a lot.'

'No problem.'

And clearly Jackie knew better than to argue with someone who was like a coiled spring. Back from her honeymoon and looking ten years younger, the efficient, kind, capable consultant was back. Without the endless stress of a wedding to prepare for the self-centredness was gone, and when she disappeared and came back with two mugs of coffee, she addressed not the immediate problem, but what was really going on.

'How's your father doing, Iosef?' Funny that Jackie was allowed to ask questions that *she* couldn't. That after a frantic morning in a lull between patients she could voice the words

Annie was dying to, *and* even though he was in a foul mood, even though he was snapping at everyone, despite his refusal to discuss it with her, Jackie actually managed to get an answer.

'Not so good.' Iosef rubbed his forehead and gave up on the notes he was trying to write at the nurses' station, accepting not just the mug of coffee from his boss but the chance to talk, too. 'Really, I think he should be moved to the hospice now, but my mother refuses to accept that it's near the end. She still insists that with the right treatment he's going to get better. That if he can just hold on, a cure might be around the corner. I just don't see how she can't accept it.'

Strange, Annie thought, as she continued to fill the now overflowing syringe drawer, that the only way she could find out more was to listen in on his conversation with somebody else.

'Denial's a powerful drug.' Jackie gave a sympathetic smile. 'Is there anything that we can do for you, Iosef, at this end?'

'I don't think there's anything more to be done at the moment.'

'If you want some time off, you only have to ask.'

'Thank you.'

'And you know if you want him admitted to the private wing here, you just say the word.'

'I think the private hospital is better. Not the care…' He shook his head in needless apology, in case Jackie had misunderstood. 'The press is going crazy at the moment and there, well, they're more used to dealing with them. I'm sure you don't want a load of journalists camping out in the ambulance bay.'

'I'd set the guard dogs on them.' Jackie smiled as Iosef turned his back, closing the discussion, but Jackie didn't leave it there. 'Give it some thought, Iosef—it might be nice for you to have him close. Let me know if you change your mind.'

'I will.'

'And look after yourself in the midst of all this,' Jackie added, reaching for the phone as it shrilled. 'Tell that Candy to spoil *you* for once—not the other way around.'

Annie waited for him to tell Jackie they weren't together anymore, to say something—*anything*—to slow the heart that was hammering in her chest. But he didn't.

Didn't say a single word. And as Jackie picked up the phone and started talking, for a tiny second their eyes locked. A million questions were burning in hers but each and every one was left completely unanswered as he tore his eyes away, picked up his pen to resume writing his notes. Jackie's earlier words echoed, haunting Annie now.

Denial's a powerful drug.

'We've got a newborn coming in.' Jackie put down the phone and gestured for Annie to come over, and any relationship woes were pushed firmly aside when she revealed the contents of the call. 'Apparently the baby's been found abandoned in a shopping-mall toilet.'

'I'll go and warm the cot, get things ready.'

206 BILLIONAIRE DOCTOR, ORDINARY NURSE

Annie headed for Resus, with Jackie and Iosef walking briskly alongside her.

'When you have done that, ring Security and Social Services—actually, I might just ring the nursing co-ordinator now…'

'Why?' Iosef's question had Annie frowning as she flicked on the cot and started preparing for the infant's arrival. 'Why do you need to ring the co-ordinator? We don't know the baby's condition. It might not even need an ICU bed.'

'I'm not worried about the bed state.' Jackie gave him an old-fashioned look as she punched in the co-ordinator's number. 'You know how we were just talking about the press—well, wait till they get hold of this.'

They already had.

A bystander at the shopping mall had called a talkback radio station and as Annie went out to greet the ambulance, photographers were already gathering, attempting to get shots of the baby who was being shielded by a blanket as the paramedic raced her through the department and into the resuscitation area, carefully placing her under the heater as everyone swung into action.

'The woman who found her heard a small cry but nothing really since then. She's pretty flat.'

'Hypothermic.' Iosef checked the baby's temperature then nodded as Annie delivered warm, humidified oxygen. Briskly stepping aside when the anaesthetist arrived, and having checked the baby's glucose levels, she set up the dextrose infusion Iosef had ordered. 'Two, maybe three hours old,' Iosef said, checking the status of the umbilical cord as he inserted a line to deliver drugs. 'She's very small.'

It sounded as if he was stating the obvious, but Annie knew his trained eye was stating far more. The baby was very small and scrawny, but in a newborn size and weight weren't always indicative of gestational age. He measured her head with tape then his meticulous eyes and fingers scanned and probed the newborn, noting the well-formed ears, the nipples, the creases on the soles of her feet—digesting the information before he gave his verdict. 'This baby's full term—small, but full term. Let's weigh her.'

'She's very jittery,' Annie noted as the baby started to respond to warming. Her little limbs were pinking up but tiny jerking actions were apparent and Jackie wasted no time saying what Annie was thinking.

'She could be suffering drug withdrawal, given that her mother—'

'Her blood sugar levels are low,' Iosef interrupted. 'Let's just deal with the few facts that we do know—and hypoglycaemia would more than account for her jitteriness. Where are the paediatricians?'

'Stuck on the ward with a sudden collapse,' the nurse co-ordinator answered as she came in, turning off her shrilling pager. 'Poor little mite—what an awful start to life.'

'She's fine!' Iosef's response was very matter-of-fact. 'She's responding well to warming and fluids.'

She was—the little body that had been so still

was pink and moving now, and very pleasingly she was crying loudly at the indignity of it all. And even though she continued to pick up, she was still too sick and exhausted to be bathed yet, so instead, when things had stabilised, Annie popped on a nappy and swaddled her in a bunny rug, popping a little pink hat on her head to keep her warm.

'That's better!' Iosef came over with her notes and looked down at his patient. 'She looks like a baby now.' He shook his head at his own choice of words. 'You know what I mean.'

And as curt and dismissive as he was with everyone else, he was incredibly tender with the baby. One very large finger stroked one very tiny cheek and Iosef actually smiled as the babe turned its head instinctively, rosebud lips searching for food.

'Do you want me to try the paediatricians?' the nurse co-ordinator asked. 'They could probably send down the reg.'

'Why?' Jackie's nod to the nurse co-ordinator died as Iosef frowned. 'What's the paediatrician going to do that we're not? Best that we just watch her now, let her recover from the trauma of birth. Perhaps a warm feed in half an hour if she's still stable and then the paediatricians can assess her when they are ready.' He stared down at the little girl again, his finger still by her cheek, and even if new babies couldn't focus, Annie could have sworn this little lady's eyes were attempting it with Iosef. If a tiny being less than a few hours old could warm to another human, then she was.

'Do we have a pacifier?' As Annie frowned he elaborated. 'A dummy, a nipple.'

'I don't think so.' Helplessly she shook her head. 'I can ring Maternity, but I doubt they—'

'We endorse breastfeeding here,' the nurse co-ordinator chimed in, but rapidly halted as he Iosef gave her the most ironic of smiles.

'Either you provide me with a lactating woman in the next five minutes or you find me a pacifier.'

'You'll be OK little one…' His voice was as

brusque as it was with anyone he came into contact with, only the babe didn't seem to care a jot. Her little face turned, her eyes closed as she relaxed in his hands, the IV satisfying her hunger for now. And for the first time in her little life her body was warm, all needs attended to sufficiently for her to relax.

'We'll need to talk to the press,' the nursing co-ordinator said.

'Why?'

'Well—they're outside.'

'So?'

'We need to find the mother. To let her know—'

'I'm sure she knows she's given birth,' Iosef retorted. 'And I'm sure the press has already let everyone know what hospital the baby's in.'

'The usual practice is—'

'I do not want this baby paraded on the evening news tonight.' Iosef completely overrode her. 'I do not want her paraded for everyone to see under the guise of bringing the mother forward. Am I making myself clear?'

'Perfectly!' the nurse co-ordinator answered tightly.

'Both this baby and her mother deserve better than that,' Iosef said, before stalking out.

'Does he deliberately set out to upset everyone?' the nurse co-ordinator asked Jackie as Annie checked the baby's obs. And if it seemed the sort of conversation that usually took place behind closed doors, it didn't because it was Emergency, strong personalities clashing a frequent occurence. 'I've just had a very upset nurse from the medical ward on the phone.'

'Has the bed been made for the patient yet?' Jackie asked tartly.

'We're two domestics short. We can't just drop everything because a senior registrar demands it. His patients aren't the only ones in the hospital.'

'They're *his* only ones,' Jackie flared, and Annie knew that even if she'd address the issue with Iosef, she certainly wasn't going to let the nursing co-ordinator know that. One of the many things Annie admired about Jackie was that she defended her team to the hilt. 'Don't grumble to me about a member my team without very good reason. He happens to be the best doctor we've had in this place in a long time—I know I've certainly learnt a lot from him. Now, if you'll excuse me, I've got patients to see. Perhaps you'd be kind enough to ring down when Mrs Lucas's bed is finally ready.'

It was the nursing co-ordinator's turn to stalk out now.

'Bloody Iosef,' Jackie sighed, because to Annie she could say that.

'Are you going to talk to him?'

'And say what—that he's got to stop walking around insisting he knows best?' She gave a small eye roll. 'You know what his answer would be, don't you?'

'That he does!'

'He actually does!' Jackie managed a wry smile. 'Not that I'll tell him that. OK, I'm off to pull rank. Wish me luck.'

'Good luck!'

Even with the baby moved safely to the maternity ward, the department was still kept on its toes dealing with the incident, fielding calls from reporters, even a couple of women claiming to be the mother—and even if it was a blatant hoax, each call had to be handled professionally and bounced to the appropriate authorities—the television in the staff-room blaring out the news. But it wasn't just the vile shift, the baby and her missing mother or the thirty-nine-year-old who in the end never actually made it up to the ward that occupied Annie's mind.

They'd promised to never bring their relationship to work but it took a supreme effort today to talk to him about a patient, to pass him in the corridor, to even sit with him on a quick coffee-break and not confront him.

To not ask the question she needed the answer to now.

'Annie…' Melanie's anxious face appeared

around the curtain, followed by the rest of her. 'I know you're about to go off duty, but I need a hand.'

'Sure.' Annie said as Melanie pulled her aside.

'I think I might have the baby's mum here…her parents have just gone to register her. She came home from school and has been in bed since with abdominal pain. They think she might have appendicitis, which, of course, she might— only she doesn't want to get undressed.' Melanie gave a worried shrug. 'I think you might be better with her than me, just for the initial bit— I know you've got to go soon.' And it was an honest admission that was often made in nursing—no matter how good your skills, sometimes things could be better handled by others, and Melanie was generous enough to her patient to admit that tact and dragging out information weren't her strongest points.

'Try and get the family to stay in the waiting room for now,' Annie said. 'How old is she?'

'Sixteen. Her name's Rebecca.'

'Hi, Rebecca.' Smiling as she entered, Annie walked in, saw the pale, fearful face on the pillow and was positive that Melanie was right, or even if she was wrong, there was something big going on with this young girl. 'I hear you've got a stomachache.'

'I don't need to see a doctor,' Rebecca started. 'I just want to go home.'

'You don't look very well,' Annie said, and took a deep breath. 'Look, Rebecca, I've asked Melanie, the other nurse, to keep your parents down in the waiting room for now. Is there anything you want to say—anything you want to tell me while they're not here?'

'No.'

'OK, well, I'm going to do a set of obs on you and then we'll get the doctor to come in and see you.'

'I don't want to see the doctor.'

'Rebecca, you're clearly not well. Your parents are worried about you. Now, whatever is going on, it has to be dealt with.'

'I can't,' the young girl begged. 'I just want to go home.'

'That's not going to happen,' Annie said gently, because quite simply it wasn't. Her parents were not going to turn around and drive home without their daughter being examined, and however much Rebecca might want it all to go away, some things just didn't. 'Why don't you tell me what's wrong?'

'You already know, don't you?'

'I think so.' Annie nodded.

'Is she OK?' Rebecca sobbed. 'They said on the news that she wasn't breathing.'

'She's fine,' Annie said gently, touched on the baby's behalf that it was the first thing she asked. 'She never stopped breathing—she was just a bit cold and shocked when the ambulance brought her in. Babies lose heat very quickly.'

'I rang for an ambulance for her,' Rebecca gulped. 'I know somebody found her, but I had rung for an ambulance…on the phone outside the toilets.'

'I know that, too,' Annie said. 'She's up in

Maternity now and, no doubt, being spoilt and cuddled. She's a little bit small so they're keeping a bit more of an eye on her, but she seems to be doing fine. Now we have to look after you.'

'What am I going to tell my mum and dad?'

'First,' Annie said firmly, 'I'm going to do some obs, and then have a quick look at you—then we'll get the doctor in and *then* we can work that one out.'

'Your mum and dad are in the waiting room.' Melanie came in quietly as Annie checked Rebecca, and she didn't really have to ask if she'd been right, so she didn't, just held Rebecca's hand instead. 'How are you doing?'

'Scared.'

'I'll bet.' Melanie gave her a nice smile and a little wink. 'I'll stick with you—I'm good at that!'

'She is.' Annie nodded. 'Right, I'll go and get Jackie.'

'She's in a meeting,' Melanie said. 'Try Iosef.'

'Sorry to disturb you…' Knocking on his open

door, jacket on and lanyard off, Annie forced a tired smile as she pulled out her hair-tie. 'The baby's mother has just come in. Her family brought her—they think she's just got abdo pain.'

'How is she?'

'Young, scared...' His eyes closed as she answered and stayed closed as he voiced another question.

'Did she ask after the baby?'

'First thing she did when she worked out I knew.'

'That's good,' Iosef answered, but even if it was the right response, it was so forced it made her frown, and for the first time she actually looked at him properly. His eyes were still closed in his ashen face, his breathing was rapid, and for an appalling second Annie thought he must have had bad news, that he must have found out his father had died.

'Is everything OK?'

'Fine.' He snapped to attention. 'I am just finishing...' He stood up without looking up, closing down his computer and picking up some papers. 'Has George rung the obstetrician?'

'George hasn't even been in to see her, just Melanie and I. She's literally only just come in and we thought it better if one of the senior staff see her.'

'You said she seemed OK.' It was Iosef frowning now—frowning at Annie who was staring at him. He was suddenly more remote than usual, impossible to reach, to touch, and the anger boiling inside her now was not solely on behalf of her patient. Even if every word voiced related to work, Annie knew on a deeper level, *knew* as sure as eggs were eggs, that there was another conversation going on entirely. 'George can manage her care!'

'This from a doctor who barely lets George suture his own patients, a doctor who runs around giving out drugs, policing everyone— but *now*, when a fragile woman is brought in, someone who *needs* a senior doctor…' his face was as white as chalk as she confronted him, a muscle pounding in his cheek as black eyes refused to look at her '…you're suddenly only too happy to pass the buck. What *is* your problem, Iosef?'

'Right now…' His voice was surly, eyes narrowed to two slits as he glanced at his watch. 'My problem is a terminally ill father and *his* doctor who I am supposed to be meeting in ten minutes to discuss his pain regime. You know, I have spent five years working in a place where most of the babies filling the orphanages are abandoned. Don't question me when this is something I used to deal with on a daily basis.'

'I understand that you—'

'Understand?' he interrupted her with a sneering, mirthless laugh, the black mood that had rumbled all day reaching its tipping point. 'You understand, do you? You have the temerity to stand there and say you understand how I am feeling when we had a four-year-old in this morning who had nearly drowned, we lost a thirty-nine-year-old woman to cancer at nine minutes past two—and I know the time because I was the one who wrote the death certificate.

Why isn't that on the news? Why isn't the whole department wringing their hands about that, instead of creating a circus over two relatively healthy people? Understand. This—is—nothing—new—to—me!'

'Haven't you gone yet?' Jackie, back from her meeting, popped her head around the door, her smile fading as she picked up on the thick tension in the room. 'Is everything OK?'

'I was just letting Iosef know that the baby's mother has come in.' Annie cleared her throat, her cheeks burning with anger, her throat dry at his brutal words and her heart weary with it all. Hell, she'd wanted emotion, wanted to know how he was feeling—but not like this! 'The parents don't seem to have a clue and I thought it more appropriate that a senior doctor—'

'I'll do it,' Jackie said easily, clearly assuming she now knew what was going on. 'Iosef has to dash off this evening, don't you? Anyway, it might be more comfortable for her to speak to a woman.'

'Thanks,' Iosef called to her departing back,

picking up his keys and heading to the door. He paused to wait for her to exit so he could lock up, but still she stood there. And, yes, clearly he hadn't been lying, maybe he *did* have somewhere he needed to be—but he *was* being evasive.

'I'm glad.' She could feel his impatience, *knew* he wanted her to leave, wanted this conversation to be over, but somehow she also knew that something had seriously rattled him, that on some level she didn't understand she was seeing a side of Iosef he didn't usually choose to reveal. 'I'm glad!' Annie said again, only more loudly this time, ignoring the hiss of his breath as she refused to move. 'Glad that it is on the news, glad that I live in a country that balks at the thought of anyone abandoning a baby, that still has the heart to be shocked that a parent could leave their own child—'

'Leave it!' he barked. 'Just leave it, Annie!'

'Leave what?' Annie challenged, her chin jutting defiantly, shaking as she saw that she had touched a nerve that was clearly raw and forbidden but probing it anyway. 'Oh, I'm sorry—I didn't realize. Is this *another* thing we can't discuss?'

Thankfully he closed the door—thankfully because any semblance of this being a professional difference of opinion had long since gone. And he knew that, too, turning the lock just in case Jackie, or a domestic, or another of the hundreds he insisted they lie to might stumble in on this.

This what? she screamed in her head as he came over, because even if he meant everything to her, what they had could hardly be described as a relationship. But he knocked the wind out of her again by taking the road least expected. 'Annie…' His voice was weary, a heavy mix of exhaustion and exasperation. His hands reached out for her, his fingers knotting her hair, his head burying itself in her neck, groaning her name over and over before finally revealing just a little bit more of nothing. 'I don't want to deal with my thoughts now.' He was almost pleading, his appeal toying with her soul as his mouth searched her neck, easily crossing her boundaries again as he pushed her to the desk.

His kisses were so hard they should have hurt, but she hurt anyway, her mouth searching his because it was easier than speaking, easier than voicing what had to be asked, easier for his lips to deliver release than deliver an answer she didn't want to deal with.

For now...Annie promised herself. Just for now.

She could almost glimpse the ache of withdrawal that would surely come afterwards—ravenous now for what had to be the final fix, the final bliss of oblivion before she confronted hell.

And he craved oblivion, too.

More than her even.

This aloof, remote man needed her now on a level she'd never experienced, his frantic lips still tasting her as he pushed up her skirt, his impatient fingers shredding her pantyhose, tearing at her knickers. And if it was frenzied it wasn't without sentiment. Emotionless sex was impossible with this man, Annie pulling at his clothes as frantically as he tugged at hers, opening his shirt so she could suck on his shoulder, feel the blissful scratch of his thighs against hers, touching him, tasting him, feeling him, devouring him because somehow she knew she was kissing him goodbye.

Because it was just too good and too bad and too dangerous to last, her release meeting his as he dived inside her, followed closely by tears, not at what had taken place but at what now must.

'I'll come over later.' He said it into her hair, held her tightly when he had to let go.

'Why don't I come over to you?' she offered, but it wasn't out of kindness. She closed her eyes and prayed for a yes, her eyes screwing closed as he gripped her tighter and shook his head.

'Stay with me.' His head was back in her neck, their bodies still entwined, coming down slowly from the heady rush, somehow both knowing the landing was going to be bumpy. 'Stay with me for a bit longer.'

Confusing words made sense. Annie knew he was asking her not to ask, to hold onto what they had for just a little while longer—only she couldn't.

'We should go out tonight…' Her voice was hesitant, both bodies tensing as she refused to carry on playing the game they'd started. 'Catch a movie or something…'

But still he tried.

'It's been a long day. I'll grab some take-away.'

She was really crying now, silent, wretched tears as the writing on the wall came into horrible focus. 'Why can't I come over to you?' Pulling back, she stared at his pained face, watched his mouth struggle to form an excuse, and actually wanted to slap him for what he'd made her. 'I—want—to—go—out—tonight!' Insistent words were de-livered through bitter lips. 'In the city. I want to eat out at some fabulous restaurant, slap bang under bright lights—my treat,' she spat, 'in case you're worried I'm after you for your money.'

'Annie, please…'

'You know…' Pushing him away, then peeling off shoes and shredded stockings and panties didn't make for a particularly dignified ending. Neither did a running nose when she finally managed to look at him. 'There are two reasons a man doesn't want to be seen with a woman—either he's ashamed of her or worried he's going to get caught. So which one is it, Iosef?'

'You don't understand!'

'And I'm quite sure you're about to tell me that *she* doesn't understand you either. Actually, don't even bother answering my question.' She put up a shaking hand. 'Because I don't really care which one it is. Whether or not I'm good enough for you, Iosef, I'm good enough for me—and if there is someone else, screw you!' Putting her shoes back on, she ran for the door but, forgetting it was locked, had to suffer the indignity of waiting for him to come over with his keys. But he refused to open it, prolonging the agony, prolonging the inevitable.

'Why would you think I was ashamed of you, Annie? I would give anything—'

'Open the door.'

'We need to talk.'

'OK then. I'll talk—and you can listen. Remember that "silly girl" taunt when you thought I was anorexic?'

'What the hell does that have to do with this?'

'Well, I was that *silly girl* once,' she shouted, 'when I was a teenager—counting calories, tummy crunches, hating every piece of my skin. And I feel as if I'm becoming that person again.'

'What are you talking about?'

He didn't get it—she didn't really get it. It wasn't food that was the problem, it was him, the lies she was telling herself and the lies by omission she was telling others—living a secretive existence again. 'I hate what I let you make me…trying to look perfect 24/7 in case the fabulous Iosef Kolovsky decides to drop around and ask me to drop my knickers.'

'Have I ever once put any pressure on you to look good?' His voice was breathless. It was as if she'd slapped him, her venom stunning him, his expression reeling from her confession. 'Have I ever once made you feel less than—?'

'Have you ever once been truly honest with me?'

She hated it that he couldn't answer, hated it that he screwed his eyes closed.

'Open the door!'

'Annie, this is not about how you look,' he attempted, but she shook her head.

'Take me out tonight, then.'

'I can't.'

'But you'll take Candy out?'

'Candy and I… It's complicated…' And on cue his phone rang. Whether or not it was Candy, Annie knew that it often had been and she almost *did* slap him then, her hand actually lifting as his teeth gritted for the impact, his lying eyes pleading for understanding when she found out she couldn't resort to violence. 'Annie, if you'll just calm down for a moment.'

'Calm down!' Her hand clamped over her mouth instead of his cheek, her eyes livid, the incredulous laugh that shot from her lips bordering on hysterical as the phone that had gone silent for a few seconds started trilling again. And she realised what she'd become as she dragged her hand down and rattled at the door.

'You'd better answer your phone—someone clearly needs to talk to you.'

'She can wait!'

'Well, I can't.' Annie retorted. 'I swear to God, Iosef, if you don't unlock the door this second, I'm going to scream!'

And even if he *was* unlocking the door now, even if it was opening and she was running out, it was like being thrown into prison, a prison of her own making—the sentence for her crime never more evident as Melanie swung out of the mini-kitchen with a tray of coffee for Rebecca's family.

'Annie, are you still here?' Her friendly greeting faded, concern etched on her face as she took in Annie's tear-streaked face. 'What on earth happened?'

'Nothing.'

'You're crying!'

Worse than prison, Annie thought, she'd been placed in solitary.

'It's just been one helluva shift,' Annie attempted. 'You know, Mrs Lucas the baby and her mum—I guess it just gets to you sometimes.'

'I'll come over,' Melanie offered. 'As soon as my shift ends.'

'No.' Annie shook her head and lied to her friend because she had to. 'I'd really rather be alone.'

CHAPTER TWELVE

For Annie it was excruciating to sit in the staff-room where she'd once been so comfortable and attempt to groan about the weather or empty coffee-jar. Hell, to talk to him about a patient, or work alongside him, and just, just... *unbearable* to have to walk into his office on occasion and not remember what had taken place on his desk.

'These are the files you wanted.' She couldn't look at him and couldn't look at the desk either, couldn't even put the notes down where her bottom had been, so instead, taut with tension, she sort of thrust them at him.

'Thank you. Annie, could we—?'

'Jackie wants everyone in the staffroom in

fifteen minutes.' Annie cut him off as she always did when he tried to talk to her about them.

'She is going to announce that I'm being offered the consultant's position.'

'Congratulations.'

'If it is a problem for you…'

'There are a million exe's working alongside each other—I'm sure we can manage to remain civil!' Annie snapped, thankful for Melanie's unwitting words. Maybe there were, as Melanie had said, a million exes working alongside each other and managing to be civil, but on reflection maybe she was wrong.

A working relationship with someone you'd had a personal relationship with wasn't an ideal scenario.

'Even so,' Iosef said, 'if it is going to be a problem for you, I need you to tell me—preferably before the announcement's made.'

'Oh, so you'd turn it down for me?' Annie scoffed.

'You were here first. Morally I feel—'

'Morally…' Annie actually managed to laugh. 'You're very good at saying the right thing, but we both know you've got the morals of an alley cat!'

'Annie, please…'

'Get over yourself, Iosef.' Annie turned for the door. 'I already have.'

Brave words perhaps, and they both knew she was lying.

Both knew she didn't hate him, because it was hard to hate a person you loved. Harder when that person seemed to be fading before her eyes. As the days moved endlessly on, the dashing, cocky, arrogant doctor who had swept her off her feet and out of her mind seemed somehow diminished now.

His face was grey with tension, exhaustion seeping from him as he dragged himself through each day. Sometimes she'd stare at those broad, taut shoulders and the impulse to go over, kiss the back of his neck and massage away the tension was overwhelming. Especially as she knew that he needed it, wanted it—knew that he was weak for her, too.

Knew because her mobile and doorbell often trilled, sometimes late at night, like an addict begging for a fix, and it was safer, far safer to pull the pillow over her head, to delete his texts unread, to volunteer for a month of night duty. And as a last line of defence she washed off the tan and refused to shave her legs, because if somehow she did weaken, if somehow she did actually relent and open the door to him, it wouldn't go any further because she'd hardly let him see her like that.

The mood in Emergency was as sombre as Annie felt when she arrived for her night shift, and she headed through the darkened obs ward, the curtains pulled around a bed, Melanie giving her just a grim smile as Annie walked past. Pulling out her supper, Annie hauled her bag into her locker then put a smelly, garlic-laced curry in the fridge, so in case Iosef did get called in she'd be stinking to high heaven!

'Poor patients!'

'Talking to yourself again?' Jackie made her jump as she came in and Annie forced a smile, but it changed when she saw Jackie's tired face. 'What's wrong?'

'You haven't heard?'

'What?'

'Ivan Kolovsky was brought in this afternoon.'

'Oh.' It felt as if the marrow was seeping out of her bones—the effort of trying to remain professional *and* compassionate as she would be for any *other* colleague an almost impossible feat when it was Iosef they were talking about. 'Is he…?'

'No.' Jackie shook her head. 'But it *is* the end of the road for him. It's been a very trying evening. Iosef had been here working most of the night and all day—he was just finishing up when Ivan was brought in, so he's beyond exhausted. The plan had been for Ivan to die at home, but apparently his wife panicked. We were going to transfer him but he's just too ill to be moved.'

'So he's on the private ward?' Annie frowned, wondering why Jackie was telling her so much,

wondering why she was privy to so much information, and rather personal information, too.
Her heart thudded in her chest as realisation hit
even before Jackie answered her.

'We're trying to keep it from the press so,
rather than have him fully admitted, I've closed
off the obs wards and he'll stay here until…'

'Here!' Annie's voice was a croak, the impos-
sibility of being so close to Iosef and not able to
do anything almost more than she could bear,
only her pain hadn't touched sides yet, her head
shaking as Jackie rammed in the knife.

'Can you get the handover from Melanie?'

'Me?' She was shaking her head more firmly
now, deciding that if she had to then she would
tell Jackie the truth, positive that it would just
make this wretched night, even more miserable,
and not just for her but for Iosef, too. 'Jackie,
Iosef and I don't really get on—I'm sure he'd
prefer it if someone else looked after his father.'

'He wouldn't.' It was Jackie shaking her
head now.

'We're actually not talking at all at the moment,' Annie insisted. 'I can assure you that he won't want me—'

'Annie…' Jackie actually held her hands as she spun into panic and for the first time Annie wondered if somehow she'd actually guessed what had been going on. 'Iosef actually asked if it could be you that looks after him.'

Why?

Heading back to the obs ward, her mind screamed the question. Why would he do this to them, to her? Why would he put her through this?

'You look shocking!' Melanie greeted her in a low voice at the small desk.

'I've felt better!' She was near to tears, *desperate* to confide in someone, to pull her friend into the loo and spill the whole sorry tale. Only she couldn't , so instead Annie took a deep breath and gave a nod. 'Let's do handover.'

'Ivan Kolovsky, fifty-seven years of age…' She tried to concentrate as she heard about his long struggle with cancer, the secondaries in his brain, tried to convince herself she should be hearing this when Melanie spoke about the family, yet all the time she felt as if she were peeking through a keyhole, an intruder who really shouldn't be there. 'There's loads of relatives.' Melanie rolled her eyes. 'I've given up trying to limit numbers. There's more pacing outside, all chatting on mobile phones—I've given up telling them about the phones, too. Basically…' Melanie took a deep breath '…he's in a lot of pain, it's quite horrible to watch…'

'So why hasn't he had more morphine?' Annie frowned, peering at his drug chart. 'He's written up for it PRN, there's no reason for him to be in pain.'

'He's waiting for his son to get here from the UK—Levander. He was actually on his way anyway when all this happened, so the poor guy doesn't know yet just how sick he is. Aleksi, one of the other sons, has gone to meet him from the airport. His plane should get in around eleven, so hopefully Ivan can hold on till then.'

'He shouldn't be in pain!' Annie insisted.

'He wants to talk to his son…' Melanie gave a helpless shrug. 'He says there's something he needs to say.'

'How's Iosef?' She tried to say it normally, tried to voice the question as she would have if it were any other colleague this was happening to, but her voice strangled in the middle, though Melanie didn't seem to notice.

'Grim. There's some serious stuff going down with that family for sure. Iosef is hardly talking to his mother—his father either, come to that. In fact, he's spent more time outside with Aleksi than in here. He's gone to lie down now in the on-call room. We're to call him if there's any change or when Levander's plane lands.'

'Anything else?'

'Loads, probably,' Melanie sighed. 'But that should get you through— Oh, there's a daughter, too—Annika. She's going to go to bits when it happens, just so you know.

'I'll turn him with you before I go.'

'Thanks.'

'You're OK with all this?'

'Me?' Annie tried a don't-be-daft smile. 'I'm fine.'

'Really?'

'Really.'

'Only I haven't seen you much these past few weeks and…' Melanie stood up, gave Annie's shoulder a bit more than a friendly squeeze. 'Ring me if you need to.'

'I will.' Annie nodded. 'I'll try and give you a buzz when I wake up tomorrow.'

'I meant tonight.'

Ivan's family were *exceptionally* difficult. They just couldn't fathom, despite Annie's and Melanie's patient explanations, why they had to move him when it was surely going to make his pain worse, why they had to wash and turn him when he was already suffering enough.

'His skin's so fragile at the moment, he'll be *more* sore if he's left in one position. I know it seems cruel, but he honestly needs it—we've already stretched the time between turns as much as we can.'

Annie could see their point, though. Hearing him yelp and whimper in pain, no matter how gently they washed and turned him, brought a sting of tears to her eyes, but the pain of movement in this case was better than being left to lie still. Just because a body was ceasing to live, it still functioned.

'*Gede?*' Fading grey eyes held hers as over and over he used a word that was said with such desperation and pleading it didn't need translating.

'Soon, Ivan,' Annie and his family repeated a hundred times over the next few hours. 'Levander will be here soon.' Eyes turning and looking at the clock, praying that Aleksi would ring with news that Levander's plane had landed. And though on a humane note it was all Annie wanted for her patient, on a personal level, when at midnight the news came that Levander and his wife Millie had cleared customs with their new baby Sashar, Annie closed her eyes as she knocked on the doctors' on-call room, tried like she never had before to somehow be professional as she stepped in.

'Your brother's on his way—they should be here in half an hour or so.'

'Has my father had any morphine yet?'

'He's still refusing—he says he needs to speak to Levander.'

'I'm sorry.' She could hardly see him in the dark room, which helped, the pain behind his strong voice making her want to hold him. To be able to see that pain in his eyes too would be the last straw.

'Don't worry about that now. Just concentrate on tonight.'

'I'm sorry about tonight, for asking for you to nurse him. I know it must be hell for you…'

'Don't worry about me, Iosef. I'm fine.' She turned to go, nails biting into her palms as he called her back.

'I need to tell you something—and you're the only person here I think I can tell. It's about my father. My brother—if the person looking after him can understand...' And she didn't want to hear it, yet really she had no choice, and she took the deepest breath before flicking on the light then she walked over, sat on the edge of the on-call bed and gave a nod, hating it that he was still pulling her in deeper, promising herself that tomorrow she'd start to dig herself out again.

'My mother, Nina, is not Levander's mother.'

'OK.' Staring down at her skirt, she pleated the hem between her fingers.

'My father had a brief fling with his cleaner, I think before he married my mother—I'm really not sure—but when my mother was pregnant with Aleksi and I, they left Russia to come here.'

'So Levander stayed behind?' Annie checked, 'with his mother?'

'It didn't work out like that. Very soon after they left, Levander's mother died, only my parents apparently didn't know...'

'Apparently?'

'He sent money back, he wrote letters, only it turned out that Levander never got them.'

'Maybe communication was difficult… And if her family…'

'From the age of three he was raised in an orphanage.' He halted her with the terrible truth. 'He lived through hell, Annie.'

'That's why the abandoned baby upset you so much, why you didn't want to deal with his mother…' Annie gulped as she recalled his outburst that day, understood now why he hadn't wanted to deal not just with the mother but with his own thoughts.

'My own brother, inadvertently perhaps but unforgivably carelessly, was abandoned. Raised in a *detsky dom* with nothing, and no one even knew. We didn't know about him till he was a teenager and he came to live with us.'

She rued her own words—the spite that had been in her voice as she'd taunted him that she was glad to live somewhere that balked at a parent turning their back on their child.

'I'm sorry!' She shuddered out an apology. 'Sorry for him and sorry for you and for the terrible things that I said.'

'You didn't know,' Iosef responded. 'No one knows—it's one of our many family secrets.' And she wasn't looking at her hemline any more but at him, listening as he told her about his pain.

'I could never look at him when he came to live with us—he was angry, hostile and I just felt guilty. I tried to talk to him, only not hard enough—I guess I didn't really want to hear what he had to say. I didn't really want to know what he had been through because it made me feel worse. Made me hate my parents more than I already did. The only time I have been able to look at him is since he married Millie. For the first time I could see that he was happy, that someone understood him. She knows more about my family than I do.'

'I don't understand.'

'She knows his past—I don't, not really. I know that she was able to listen to him, that he was able to talk to her—which is something I have not been able to do. Though I am working on it.' He gave a wan smile. 'Since he got married he has opened up a bit. We talk on the phone a lot and sometimes we talk about my work in Russia and we touch on the problems in the family and I think he is starting to accept that I do care—that, in fact, since the day he came to live with us, even if I didn't show it, I have been on his side.'

'Does there have to be sides?' Annie asked. 'Your parents have to live with their mistakes—it must be hell for them, too.'

'Nowhere near my brother's hell. You grow up thinking you parents are perfect and then slowly you find out that they are not, you start to question things…'

'But they didn't *know* he was in an orphanage.'

'They chose not to.' For the first time in ages they actually looked at each other. 'I have seen first hand how my brother would have lived and what he must have endured. I know, *I know* that, no matter the excuses, no matter the reasons, what happened to Levander was wrong—he is my father's son, his firstborn, and he turned his back on him. I have known it was wrong since the day Levander came into our lives and it has been confirmed to me every day since. But this is not about me.' Frustrated, he ran a hand through his hair. 'Look after my brother and his wife. I am asking you to understand that this is so hard on them.'

'It's hard on everyone,' Annie attempted, but Iosef shook his head.

'It is harder on them—please, look out for them.'

'I will.' Annie nodded. 'Come on, come and see him.'

'I'll wait here till Levander arrives.'

'You need to go out there, Iosef. I know you're exhausted, I know this is hard, but you need to be with your dad.'

'I don't know what to say to him. I don't know if I can really forgive him.'

Oh, God, why was this so hard? Annie took his hand and urged him into action. 'Even if you can't forgive him in this lifetime, you at least need to be with him.'

'What he did was so wrong.'

'I know, or I think I know—but right now it isn't morphine your dad needs, it's his sons, and there aren't enough hours left in his life to solve everything. But you know as well as I do that if you don't go in there and, right or wrong, tell him that you love him, you're going to regret it for the rest of your life.'

'Even if I don't respect him—even if what he did sickens me…'

'Yes!' She wasn't even trying to be professional now. Tears were coursing down her cheeks as she begged him to get what she was just realizing for herself. 'Because people make mistakes, they do the most terrible, unforgivable things, but it doesn't mean you don't love them.' And that was the truth, because even if she loathed what he had made her, even if it was hard to love herself right now, she still loved *him*—remote, distant, cheat that he might be.

But some of his behaviour could be explained by his confession and she silently swore that never again would she be so quick to judge things on appearances only.

Staring down at him, she couldn't not reach over and kiss him—couldn't not take away a bit of his pain, even if it added to hers—a slow, unhurried kiss because it was going nowhere, a kiss that tasted of pain that could be dissolved for a second. His tongue stroking hers, chasing away for a moment or two all their regrets.

'Go out and be with your dad.'

He didn't nod or say yes, but when Annie stood up so did he.

'Look after my brother and his wife,' he said as he took a big breath before following her out.

'Look after yourself!'

Death *was* horrible.

Expected or sudden—nothing could truly prepare you for loss. But Annie tried. Tried to be strong with this tortured family.

'He waited for you.'

Nina, Ivan's wife, spoke as Levander came in with his wife and baby—those devilish good looks that had graced many a magazine and bedside table still apparent despite the hellish pain etched on his features, his arm wrapped tightly around his wife.

And Annie vowed again she'd try to judge less—realised that you never really knew what went on in others' lives.

She'd read about Levander Kolovsky's exploits in the past—had giggled at his playboy ways. Had always assumed he was an emotional lightweight—a spoilt rich boy who'd grown into a spoilt rich man.

Aleksi guided them to the bedside. And Iosef had been right, because though his twin looked the same, spoke the same, and was to everyone else a carbon copy of his twin, it *wasn't* Iosef.

Iosef was the one she watched as Levander hugged his father. Thick words were spoken, and it didn't matter that it was in Russian, because anyone present could hear the love and regret with each hoarse word. Later, close to crying herself, but with Iosef's instructions drilled into her mind, when Levander's wife Millie started to get restless and it looked as if at any second she might either explode or collapse, Annie took the tiny baby from the fragile-looking woman and guided her to the empty plastic chairs outside.

'He's just had morphine. He isn't in any pain now…'

'Lucky him, then!' The venom that shot from Millie caught them both by surprise, her eyes widening in horror at her own caustic words, her hand shooting over her mouth as she started to cry. 'I'm sorry. You don't need this…'

'It's OK,' Annie said gently.

'No, it's not.' Millie shook her head. 'I'm trying so hard to be strong for Levander, I know he looks like he's OK, but he's bleeding inside. I've known this day was coming for ages, I just don't think I can stay in there and make the right noises.' Pale lips shivered out words. 'I hate what he did to Levander and I hate that woman more.'

'Nina?'

'I don't want to go into it.' She shook her head. 'I can't go into it.'

'You don't have to say anything you don't want to.' Annie said. 'Just tell me what you want to do.'

'I don't think I can be nice to her. Maybe tomorrow, maybe when it's over, but I really don't think I can go in there and listen to Ivan absolve himself.'

'So stay here, then,' Annie said patiently—and the time she was taking with Millie, the words she was saying, really had nothing to do with Iosef's plea to take care of his brother and wife. Families fraught with tension, the end of an imperfect life and the fallout for everyone, was something Annie was only too used to dealing with.

'I should be there for Levander.'

'Whether you're standing with him or not, you *are* there for Levander—he knows that. It might make it easier on him if he doesn't have to worry about you getting upset.'

'Do you think so?'

Annie didn't know what to think but she did know that despite Iosef and Millie's revelations she hadn't even scratched the surface of the pain that ran through this family. But for the moment staying away seemed the best course of action for Millie. 'I have to go in and check on Ivan now. I'll take you to the staffroom and you can make yourself a coffee or something. I'll pop in on you every now and then and let you know what's happening.'

It was the longest night of her life—just wretched and difficult from the very start as they struggled to get to the end, but, turning Ivan just before dawn, Annie knew it was for the last time and, though she couldn't be certain, she explained to Nina afterwards that it looked as if the end was close.

'You shouldn't be alone, Iosef.' Nina looked over at her son, for once not speaking in Russian. 'Why don't you call Candy?'

'I'm fine.' He shook his head as Annie, seated at the desk nearby, froze, but Nina was insistent. 'Call her and tell her to come—she should be here for you.'

Of course his mobile was dead, so he had to use the desk phone and she had to sit there, tears plopping on the notes she was pretending to write as Iosef asked for Candy to come.

'She's on her way.' His voice was flat. 'She'll be fifteen minutes or so.'

The tension was unbearable for everyone, and Nina, who'd been at Ivan's side since his admission, left to get some fresh air. Although Annie understood that she must need a break, she was tempted to tell her not to go. Ivan was in Cheyne-Stokes breathing now—every delayed laboured breath—possibly his last.

Annie willed her shift to end before Ivan died, willed herself to hold it together for a few more hours, but she only succeeded in the latter. Biting into her lip as Millie bravely came in for the very end and held Levander, she tried not to watch as

Candy sobbed on Iosef's chest, and was grateful to Jackie, who came round to the obs ward and was there to help at the end.

'Come…' Nina spoke to Millie when everything had been said and done. 'You come to our house now and stay with us.'

'We're going to a hotel tonight. I think it would be…' Levander's voice broke as he spoke and Millie took over for him.

'A hotel would be better.' Supremely polite, she remained adamant. 'We didn't bring a portable cot or anything.'

'You two,' Iosef interrupted, and then glanced down at the sleeping baby she was holding, 'I mean, you three can come to my apartment if you like. When I knew you were coming I went and bought a cot and some bits for Sashar. If a hotel is better for you, though, that is fine—I understand. But you're welcome to stay any time.'

'We'd love to come and stay with you.' Millie gave a pale smile. 'Thank you, Iosef. And thank you, too, Annie, you've been marvellous.'

Levander shook her hand and said the same, so too did Aleksi and, so heartbreakingly did Iosef. 'Thank you, Annie.'

She didn't see them to the door—didn't even look as they all walked out into the early morning, just stiffened her spine and summoned her last dregs of energy and dealt with Ivan and the pile of paperwork. When the porters came for him, even though it was an hour till her shift ended, without even offering an explanation, Annie picked up her bag and buzzed on the intercom over to Section A and informed the sister in charge that she was going home.

Her work was done.

Now she somehow had to get on with her life.

CHAPTER THIRTEEN

ONLY it wasn't that easy.

As an emergency nurse Annie dealt with death on a daily basis, had even dealt with colleagues' family members on occasion—but the events that had taken place had shaken her to her very core. To be so close to the man she loved and to be able to do nothing had been unbearable. To see him, to see the *other* woman, to watch as Iosef held in his arms the woman he had cheated on with her, sickened Annie to the stomach. Yes, she had nursed Ivan well and had helped Millie, but she was angry too. In Iosef's eyes she had been the best person for the job…but had he never stopped to think…

At what cost to her?

It was stupid to take a couple of nights off sick before her off-duty days—stupid because, no doubt, Iosef wouldn't return to work after the funeral and they could be better utilised to avoid him then. But she simply couldn't face it.

For the first time in the longest time Annie picked up the phone and prepared to make her excuses, but so shocked was Beth on the end of the line at Annie's strangled, weary voice that she all but sent an ambulance. 'Take as long as you need,' Annie was told. 'That flu bug is just dire.'

Not half as dire as the Kolovsky bug!

The trouble with loving someone from a famous family was that she couldn't even turn to her horoscope in the newspaper without seeing some reference to them. Couldn't turn on the television without some newsreader telling her that Ivan Kolovsky's will would be read after the funeral—the funeral for which Melbourne was delightedly preparing. Every supermodel and actress who had ever donned a Kolovsky dress seemed to be flying in and with the supersexy Levander Kolovsky back in town, every supermodel and actress was, no doubt, hoping that same dress would rapidly come undone!

'No chance,' Annie said to herself a couple of days later, feeling relatively better, sitting in her cheeky monkey pyjamas with a tub of ice cream and a box of tissues and watching the early evening news. Snippets of the funeral showed Levander, his arm wrapped tightly around his wife, against a mass of black suits and dark sunglasses. Again, she was struck that when the camera turned on Aleksi, not for a second did she think it was Iosef, her mind welcoming the temporary distraction of trying to work out what made them different…and utterly unable to define it till Iosef came in to view, comforting Candy as she sobbed in his arms. Annie's rose-coloured glasses snapped on and she gazed at him through the raw, painful eyes of unrequited love.

That was what made him different.

She loved him.

She had played the most dangerous of games and lost, and Annie knew, as the doorbell rang, that she had no one to blame for her pain except herself.

She knew it was Iosef.

Didn't even need to open the door to know who was on the other side.

Only, unlike the last few days, now she was actually strong enough to face him—strong enough to hear whatever it was he had to say and confident enough in herself to know that, whatever his request, whether Candy was in his life or not, her answer would be no. She didn't want to live with the mistress's curse of never, ever being able to trust him.

'Haemorrhoids!' It was perhaps the strangest of greetings, but she knew his humour because he knew hers and she actually managed a smile.

'I know.'

'How?'

'Because Mickey came in when I was on nights and told me so himself.'

'I just wanted to clear a few things up.'

'Well, thanks for the wind-up.'

'Again, I couldn't resist it. In Russia...' his eyes were squinting slightly, his face greyer than it had appeared on television '...it is a custom on a day such as today to drink until you drop.'

'Well, you can have a cup of tea, then,' Annie said tightly, 'because you're not dropping here. Come in.'

'I heard you had flu.'

'I did,' Annie answered as they headed to her lounge room. And it wasn't that much of a lie because flu made you feel as if you'd been hit by a train, flu made your eyes and nose weep, made you forget about food and just want to curl up and die. 'But I'm getting over it now—in fact, I'm feeling a whole lot better.'

'That's good.' He sat down, let out such a long breath he should really have turned blue, before finally he looked at her. 'I don't want to drop because then it really is over. When I wake up tomorrow—'

'It is over, though,' Annie answered. She could double talk as easily as he. 'As hard as it is to face, there's nothing that can be done to change that.'

'I don't want to wake up tomorrow without you.'

'As I said, there's nothing that can be done to change that,' Annie said in a voice that wasn't quite as strong but still very credible. 'Iosef, did you listen to anything that I said when I ended it?'

'That is why I am here. Now I'm asking that you listen to me.'

'I don't think there's anything left to say.'

'One thing…' Adamant, he faced her. 'I just want to make one thing very clear, to be honest.' He closed his eyes at her soft mirthless laugh. 'It is imperative that you believe this. I would have been proud to have you with me today—I would have given anything to have had you by my side through all of this, and nothing would have made me happier than to take you out for dinner that night. You are without a doubt the most beautiful woman I have ever known.'

'I'm expected to believe that from a Kolovsky.'

'You have to believe that. Whatever has gone on, whatever mistakes have been made, I need you to understand that never, not for a moment, was it about you or your looks—and, given what you told me about your past, it is imperative that you understand that.'

'I'd already worked that one out, thanks.'

'It was me with the problem, not you.'

'I'd worked that one out, too.' And she sounded so convincing, Annie almost believed herself—almost, but she could still recall the dread she'd felt as she'd stepped back on the hamster wheel of attempting to attain and retain the unattainable. 'Look, Iosef, I'm not a teenager now. I chose to ignore the warning signs and I take full responsibility for getting involved with someone—'

'Full?'

'I'm fully responsible for my own actions—the same way you are for yours. I just don't want to be the person I was starting to become—ignoring my conscience, trying to look good enough, trying to keep up with the image you had of me at the wedding. That wasn't me—'

'Annie,' he interrupted sharply, 'you seem to have it in your head that I fell in love with you at the wedding.' It was like having needles stuck into her, millions of needles that pierced every fragment of her being—the only word she wanted to hear from him the one she *had* to ignore. 'It was the Monday before that—at eight minutes to twelve actually. I remember the time because I had some blood gases to do. I was just about to get up and then in you waltzed and the whole room lifted—actually, not just the room…' He gave a very wry smile. 'So perhaps it was lust then… Love, however inconvenient it was for me, came rapidly later. I was particularly horrible to you because I didn't want to get to know you. Hell, they could have spray-tanned you green with purple spots and I'd have been crazy about you. I was particularly angry with you for not eating, because I cared about you…'

He shook his head helplessly. 'I did not want to come to the wedding. I did not want to get involved with you. I offered to swap with Marshall, but he refused. He had been to the service, he said, and I should go to the reception.'

'Why didn't you want to go?'

'Because of what I knew might happen.'

'Did happen.'

'Annie, there's nothing between Candy and I.'

'Don't.' She jumped to her feet. 'Don't go there, Iosef. I don't care if you ended it tonight, I don't care if it was almost over...'

'We were never together.' He watched as she shook her head, eyes half-closed, a tired smile on her face at the futility of it all, that still he thought she might believe his lies.

'Do you think I'm weak or stupid? I've seen you together!' Her voice was rising, anger fizzing through her body now. 'I was there when your own mother—'

'Have you ever heard my mother address me in English?' He halted her tirade with a meaningless question. 'The one time she spoke to me in English it was for your benefit.'

'*My* benefit?' Annie gave a perplexed frown. 'I don't what you're talking about.'

'So that appearances were kept up, so that when the nurse spoke to her friends, or to the press or to anyone, she would say that Candy was Iosef's girlfriend.'

'And she is.' Annie started, then stopped, a tiny glimmer of something appearing in her mind, something so impossible, so improbable she shot it down in a second, didn't even give it a second glance, just blasted him with the facts.

'Your own mother sent for her, your own mother said that you needed to be with her. She rings you all the time, turns up at work crying and begging to see you. You left me the morning after the wedding and went to lunch with her— I saw the photo in the paper—and you lied to me and said that it was old!' She was shouting at him now, hurling the facts that at the time she'd tried so hard not to see! Hurled them at him so the truth might hurt him as much as it had hurt her.

'I took her to see my father.'

And the vision she'd glimpsed was taking shape now—taking impossible shape, before he even said the words.

'Candy is my father's mistress...*was* my father's mistress.' And Annie's world stopped for a few moments while everyone got off and she was left standing there, her mouth opening, eyes widening as she stepped in the impossible place Iosef inhabited. 'My father has always kept a mistress...' He just stood there and said it as she just stood there and tried to take it in. 'My mother turned a blind eye...'

'But, surely, I mean, how did your mother put up with it?'

'We don't have those sorts of conversations in our family. We don't talk about our failings or our fears—we just deny, deny, deny. We just cover our tracks and bury whoever is in our way.'

'Not you,' Annie whispered.

'Yes, me.' He nodded. 'Because I put you through hell all those weeks.'

It was too much to take in, her mind too muddled to even feel relief at the fact that he and Candy had never been involved with each other. 'Why on earth couldn't you tell me?'

'How "on earth" could I?' His eyes held hers. He let the question sink in for a moment before he elaborated. 'I kept telling myself to ignore her, not to go there, just to wait until…' He swallowed hard. 'It was not my secret to tell—and one secret revealed leads to another. At what point do you land someone with all your baggage, Annie? At what point do you trust someone enough to tell them secrets that are also other people's secrets? I trust you now, but then… That night, when the baby was abandoned, I came so close to telling you, I actually thought you might even understand, but when you said it didn't matter anyway, that I made things worse for you, I just couldn't go through with it.'

'I wasn't just talking about my body, or

keeping up appearances…' Annie shook her head in disbelief that he couldn't see it. 'Iosef, I thought you were seeing Candy.'

'I should have told you.'

'Yes!' She blinked back at him but her certainty changed to a frown as she saw things from his perspective. How *could* he? Their relationship had hit like a thunderbolt without warning, ripped into their lives with no time to prepare and she recalled the first time they'd made love, the slightly desperate note in his usually strong voice as he'd stared up at her. *'Why now Annie? Why do you do this to me now?'*

Love *had* come along when they'd least expected it.

'So did you always know about the other women? Did your mum not mind?' She closed her mouth on a stupid statement—could still see Nina in her mind's eye on the night her husband had died, a woman who had refused to leave her husband's side, taking a breath of fresh air to allow the man she loved time with the other woman he had loved, too. Of course she'd minded…of course she had. And yet somehow, deep in grief and anger, she'd put her husband first.

It really wasn't for her to judge.

'I remember rows when I was a child, knew my father had upset my mother at times…' Iosef filled in the silence, explanations coming that now weren't really needed. 'But when I came back for Levander and Millie's wedding it was clear my father did not have much longer to live and when he started to get sicker, we were talking one night and I asked him if there was anything I could do for him.' He gave a wry smile. 'I wasn't really prepared for what he asked. It turned out that Candy wanted to see him and he wanted to see her. Reputation is everything to my family—the last thing they wanted was the press exposing the affair. What the world sees and what actually happens are two entirely different things with my family. My father was too ill to drive one night, so I did—that was how it started really. There was a small piece in the paper that I had come back from Russia and was dating her, and it sort of blew up from there. We never actually sat down and discussed it, but from that day on sometimes my mother would suggest I bring Candy over, or Candy would come and see me and ask if I would mind taking her for lunch…'

'I wish you'd been able to tell me,' Annie said, 'but I understand why you couldn't.' Like a reflex gesture, just a bodily reaction that happened whether you wanted it to or not, she reached for his hands. 'No more secrets.' She frowned at his wry expression..

'I said the same to Levander this morning.' Grey eyes that had enthralled her from the start were moist. 'He told me that, yes, there were things I would never know, things I really didn't need to, and finally I can accept that. If he can accept the past, then so can I, so long as from now on…'

'You make it right.'

'We all make it right.'

'We will.' She managed a tiny laugh. 'So I'm not your mistress.'

'No.'

'So my moral character is intact!'

'Technically,' Iosef said, and Annie gave a wobbly smile.

'And your moral character?'

'Don't go there.' He smiled mischievously.

'Don't you ever go there,' Annie countered, 'because I swear I'd never be so forgiving again.'

'I love you.'

It wasn't a revelation, more an acknowledgement and one she accepted—love an impeccable excuse for irrationality, be it his or hers. Love the wobbly barometer that fluctuated at will, that blurred every line and always had you coming back for more.

'I really didn't want to love you…' He held her hand as he insulted her, that glint of mischief back in his eyes. 'I really did not want to like you—there could not have been a worse time for you to appear in my life. You walked into that staffroom and walked out with my heart.'

'I didn't.' Annie giggled.

'You did,' Iosef countered. 'And I *loathed* you for it.'

'I loathed you, too.' She kissed his proud face.

'There is something else I need to tell you.' Like a ride on a roller-coaster, her heart soared and then sank. 'I told Jackie about us.'

And duly soared again.

'You told Jackie!'

'I did not intend to—but when my father was brought in I was just…' He gave a hopeless shrug. 'I think I needed to talk to someone.' And, Annie realised, what came as naturally as breathing to her was completely alien to him. 'I offered her my resignation. I honestly thought I'd messed up your life—was worried you were about to leave—and it didn't seem fair when you were there first. When, until I came along, you were happy there.'

'And what did she say?'

'That I should wait till well after the funeral to make any big decisions. I know it sounds crazy but it was the first time I really understood that there would soon be a funeral.'

'Not crazy.' Annie shook her head.

'I told Jackie that I wanted you looking after my father and she said no. She thought, given the little I had told her, that it would be too much for you.'

'So how come I ended up looking after him?'

Iosef closed his eyes. 'I told her I loved you.'

'You told Jackie that?' And she sounded angry, only she wasn't—just stunned, so stunned that he would actually say that, not to her but to Jackie. That this remote, proud man had left himself so completely open. 'And what did she say?'

'That she'd think about it. I'm not sure if she discussed it with Melanie, but later she came and said that she was sure, if you knew that I loved you, that you'd want to do it for me.'

'So who else knows?' Annie asked. 'I mean, is there a notice up in the staffroom?'

'Maybe George…' Iosef reluctantly relented. 'I didn't tell him, but he took me out for a drink yesterday and tried to cheer me up.' He caught her eye and they managed a tiny giggle. 'I know I give him a hard time, but he really is the most self-doubting person I have ever come in to contact with. He spent most of the time apologising for wasting my time!'

And whoever said friends weren't important had never had one—this little army of people who cheered you loudly from the sidelines or quietly from behind the scenes when it was needed.

'Did you know I collect foreign coins?' Annie asked, smiling.

'Sorry?'

'I have a little jar on my dressing-table and every time I get one in my change I pop it in.'

'And?'

'I *did* think about leaving, Iosef, for a while there. Yes, I did consider it, but you need to know this—I'm dizzy and I'm emotional and I absolutely love you, but I'm also tough. I *can* live without you. I might go off to lick my wounds now and then, but I will always come back fighting.'

'And what does this have to do with coins?' A markedly bemused smile was appearing on his face.

'I never knew why I kept them, I just did.'

'And?'

'I decided this morning that I was going to throw them in the brown envelope that came around if you and Candy got married.'

'You'd have stayed?'

'I like my life, Iosef. I've worked hard to get to where I am and I'm never going to walk away from it. It would just be very nice if you were here beside me.'

'And you really love me?' Iosef checked.

'Absolutely.' Annie nodded. 'Now that I know that I can. I love you because you're so horrible and rude but you still make me laugh. I love you because—and I'm sorry if it's shallow—you're fabulous in bed and make me think that I am, too. And I love you because…' She wasn't laughing now and she wasn't crying. The moral gauge that had wobbled for so long now finally settled as she found her truth—not today's truth but finally accepting all that had come before and knowing, *knowing* she could deal with all that lay ahead. 'Somehow I knew that we were better than that—somehow I knew I was too… Somehow I knew that you really loved me.'

'And I do.'

Which was fab and everything, but he was playing with the top of her pyjamas, the kisses that were raining on her face becoming just a touch more insistent now—and because there could be no more secrets, because she'd insisted on it, Annie had to make time for one last confession.

'I don't have a body image problem.'

'Good…' Every button was open now, his lips nuzzling her breasts, his fingers stealing down her waist towards the darkest female secret of them all. 'Because your body's fantastic…'

'Just…' she wriggled an inch, frantic eyes catching his as love swept in and *again* caught her totally unprepared '…a teeny-weeny body-hair issue at the moment…'

'Try…' he said, slipping down her pyjama bottoms and sending her straight to a heavenly torture. 'Try, try and try again, and never will you turn me off.'

'Never?' Annie checked.

'Never,' Iosef affirmed.

EPILOGUE

IT SHOULD seem the strangest of weddings but for Annie it was perfect.

If they wanted Levander and Millie to be there—which they did—then it had to be quick, and given they had just buried Ivan, it had to be low key.

Low on preparation but high on love.

Everyone they cared for, and didn't really, crammed the registry office and the fabulous dinner afterwards. Annie's sisters pursing their lips in jealousy yet trying to smile; her parents utterly bemused and trying not to show their surprise that their dizzy, kind but not exceptionally gifted daughter had actually been the one who had rocketed them up in social status.

'They're wondering what on earth you see in

me!' Annie smiled as her entire family stared open-mouthed at the very happy couple.

'You've got it the wrong way round,' Iosef countered, but Annie shook her head and laughed.

'Believe me, I haven't!'

'Well—more fools them, then!'

Nina made a discreet, but later well-publicised, appearance. In just a couple of weeks she seemed to have aged a decade—as if every one of her sins had caught up with her.

And despite having learned more of Nina's role in Levander's abandonment, Annie kept her promise to herself not to judge.

She gave her a hug and thanked her for coming, told her that it was lovely to see her and watched with admiration and pride as somehow Millie and Levander said pretty much the same.

Weddings, even low key, very spontaneous ones, were, though, *very* hard work.

A sort of concentration of emotions and feelings and people who were either desperate to be together or desperate to be apart.

Still, there was always a good party afterwards!

Everyone they *really* adored squeezed into Iosef's that night as Millie and Levander packed their bags in preparation for their early morning flight.

'You should have booked a hotel,' Millie chided from the bedroom, frantically trying to squeeze milk through a breast pump so she could freeze it for the flight back to the UK the next day. 'It's your wedding night and the two of you are stuck with us lot.'

'But we love you lot.'

'You'll come and see us in England?' Millie asked for the hundredth time.

'I think Iosef's already booked the flights!'

'George wants to play strip poker!' Annika, Iosef's younger sister, plonked herself on the bed. 'I think things are starting to get out of hand.'

'Talk to George!' Annie mouthed as Iosef wandered into the bedroom and promptly wandered out again.

Jackie then wandered in with a lime margarita,

Levander turned on a massive plasma TV and ignored the women who sat chatting on the bed.

'I think I made a better bridesmaid than bride…' Annie stared down at her pale lilac dress critically. 'I was really gorgeous, you know…'

'You look fab,' Millie scolded. 'I wore jeans for my wedding.'

'Poor Mum.' Annika actually laughed. 'She longs for a big white wedding, for a Kolovsky dress to be on the news. There's still me, she says sadly, and Aleksi, too, I remind her.'

On cue he entered—shuddering at the thought.

'Not a chance! Is this where the action is?' he asked, sprawling on the bed. 'Best wedding I've been to, by the way, Annie.' Then flinched as Millie dug him in the ribs. 'Well, one of the best…'

And it was family, just a crazy family that had never been like this before—one night that could never happen again, one night when for the first time they were all united.

Till Iosef came back.

'Out…' He shooed them like flies, flicked off the

television when Levander didn't budge, ushered out a giggling Annika and Jackie and even screwed on the top of Millie's bottle of breast milk as he pushed her out, too. 'If you lot don't mind, I'd actually like to spend time with my wife.'

'I don't mind.' Annie laughed when finally he turned the lock, when finally, despite the high antics outside the room, they were alone.

'You really don't, do you?'

'Not a scrap.'

'It's our wedding night,' Iosef attempted. 'It should be about us.'

'This is us…' Annie said softly, holding him close, drinking him in. 'This is about family and friends and still being able to be yourself. Anyway, we've got plenty of nights ahead when it's just the two of us—let's just enjoy them all for tonight.'

'I love you.'

He said it again for the umpteenth time, held her so close she could barely squeeze out her answer, but hearing it again there on their wedding night it was like a poultice on a wound. She just accepted the relief that came with it.

'I know that you do.'